SUMMER'S SWEET DEMISE

KATHLEEN SUZETTE

SIGN UP

Sign up to receive my newsletter for updates on new releases and sales:

https://www.subscribepage.com/kathleen-suzette

Follow me on Facebook:

https://www.facebook.com/Kathleen-Suzette-Kate-Bell-authors-759206390932120

CHAPTER 1

*S*ummertime is one of my favorite seasons. There's nothing like a beautiful blue sky with the sun shining brightly over you as you lie on the beach reading a novel. Unless, of course, it would be carving pumpkins and drinking pumpkin spice lattes in the fall. I gazed into the full-length mirror and tucked a stray lock of my long, red, curly hair behind my ear. The rest of my mop was piled on top of my head. I was wearing a cute red T-shirt with big white and blue flip-flops drawn on it, and my faded Capri jeans. My dazzling toenails were painted red, and I wore a fancy pair of brown leather sandals that allowed my toes to peek out. I was *not* going to hide my toes today. I was also not going to lie on the beach.

"Kitty!"

I turned and looked over my shoulder at my adorable eighteen-month-old granddaughter and my not-so-enthusiastic black cat, Dixie. "Get moving, Dixie, or she's going to have your tail."

Lilly giggled as she held both hands out toward her target.

"Dixie doesn't like to be chased," I reminded her.

This elicited more giggles from Lilly as Dixie darted beneath the bed. She bent to look under the bottom railing, nearly tipping over in her rush.

I scooped Lilly into my arms and spun her around as she screamed in delight. "We're going to have some fun today. We're picking wild blueberries."

"Booberries!" she echoed in between squeals of delight.

"That's right, blueberries. Mimi is going to make blueberry cheesecake. I bet you've never had blueberry cheesecake before, have you?" I moved back to the full-length mirror and held her up so she could see herself.

She pointed at her image in the mirror and babbled something unintelligible. "That is the prettiest little girl in the entire world," I answered her unasked question.

She seemed to understand and nodded. "Lilly," she said, as clear as could be.

I gasped. "Look at you! You can say your name. Why didn't your mommy and daddy tell me this? I need to know everything that's new with you." I kissed her chubby cheek.

She giggled again. "Lilly."

I chuckled and kissed her on the cheek again. I was the most blessed Mimi in the entire world. Lilly's strawberry blonde hair was curly like mine, and I wondered if it might turn a darker red as she got older. Other than the red hair, she was the spitting image of her father, who was the spitting image of his father. But her hair and the light smattering of freckles that were beginning to appear across the bridge of her nose told me she had indeed inherited some of my DNA.

"Let's get our things ready because Auntie Lucy will be here any minute."

We turned, and I caught Dixie poking his head out from underneath the bed as I carried Lilly out of the bedroom, leaving the door open a smidge behind us.

At the bottom of the stairs, I set Lilly on the floor

and headed into the kitchen. We had already had our breakfast and were just waiting for Lucy.

It was August, and the wild blueberries were ripe here in Maine. I intended to get my fair share of them before they were gone. Lucy and I had been planning this little outing for weeks, and I was excited. It was the first time Lilly would get to pick blueberries, and picking blueberries was practically a childhood right of passage in Maine.

Lilly stuck two fingers into her mouth, gently gnawing on them as she made cooing sounds. "Are you getting more teeth in?" She sighed and removed her fingers, leaving a thin telltale trail of drool on her chin. I grabbed a paper towel and dabbed at it. "That's what I thought."

There was a knock on the front door, and then I heard it open. "Allie! I'm here!"

"We're in here!"

In a moment, she walked through the kitchen door, her eyes riveted on Lilly. "Oh, my goodness! There's that beautiful girl!"

With a squeal, Lilly crossed the short distance between them and slammed into Lucy's legs, wrapping her arms around them. Lucy hoisted her up while Lilly screamed in delight. "There you are my big girl. I've been so excited to see you." She planted a big kiss on her cheek. "Aren't you dressed adorably?"

"I bought that little romper from the children's shop downtown," I said as I stowed a couple of cereal bars into a small canvas bag I was going to take with us just in case Lilly got hungry. The romper was white with yellow daisies scattered across the front and her hair was in pigtails with tiny yellow scrunchies holding them in place.

"It's darling," she said. "Look at those curls in her hair." Lucy fingered one of Lilly's pigtails, and Lilly puckered her lips for a kiss.

"Aren't you the sweetest? I swear, you can have anything you want. Anything. Just name it." She leaned over and kissed her.

I chuckled as Dixie slinked into the kitchen. He might pretend that he wanted nothing to do with Lilly, but he was constantly in her orbit. "Be careful what you promise with that one," I warned Lucy. "I have a feeling that when she's old enough to express her wants, she won't hesitate to do it."

Lucy shook her head. "No, and she shouldn't. My job is to spoil her, and that's what I'm going to do."

I grinned. Lucy and her husband Ed didn't have any children of their own, and I was more than happy to share my grandbaby with them. "All right, but don't say I didn't warn you." I grabbed two juice pouches from the refrigerator and tossed them into the canvas bag. "Now then, I've got my sunglasses, sunblock, juice, cereal bars... Oh, I think I'm going to grab some water bottles for us, just in case." I went to the refrigerator, grabbed two bottles, and stuck them in the bag.

"This will be fun. I bet Lilly will have a ball," she said as Lilly wiggled her way out of her arms and back onto the floor. She had spotted her prey.

"I know she's going to have a lot of fun. And I'm sure she's going to make a mess of herself as well. That romper had better clean up well."

Lucy chuckled and leaned on the counter. "You'll have to soak it. I'm excited about picking blueberries, too. I want to put some in the freezer, so we have some when they're out of season. There's nothing like fresh blueberries that you have picked yourself." Lucy's short blond hair poked out from beneath the pink scarf she wore, and I could smell sunscreen.

I nodded as I went to the pantry to grab some crackers for Lilly. Why was it you had to pack a tiny smorgasbord every time you took a kid somewhere? I didn't remember doing that when my kids were little, but maybe my memory was faulty. "I agree. There's nothing like wild blueberries. I can hardly wait for the cheesecake I'm going to make."

She looked at me, one eyebrow raised. "Cheesecake? As in, one cheesecake? You're going to make a cheesecake for Ed and me, aren't you? It's been a long time since you've made us one."

"Yes, I'll make one for you too, and I'll probably have to make one for Thad and Sara. Jennifer has gone back to the dorm at the college, so I don't have to make one for her." My daughter was in her last year of college, and I was grateful for that. Although it meant we were all entering a new phase of life, it was time. Those college bills added up fast.

"Oh, I can hardly wait for a taste of that sweet, creamy deliciousness," she said, grinning. Lilly toddled after Dixie, who stayed two steps ahead of her to keep his tail from being grabbed. "Look at the two of them. I'm glad they get along so well."

"Dixie pretends not to like her, but it's all a lie. How are your kittens doing?" I asked as I opened the refrigerator door and perused its contents. Did we have enough snacks? Or should I pack a few more things?

She chuckled. "Snow and Coal are the most rambunctious kittens I have ever met. Ed's constantly tripping over them, but I told him it's his fault. He needs to watch where he's going."

I looked over my shoulder at her. "Well, it couldn't be the cats' fault. It has to be his."

She nodded. "That's what I said. He tries to get me to believe that it's the two of them, but I I'll never believe it."

I chuckled and looked back into the refrigerator. Lucy had adopted two kittens last month and they were the most adorable little things ever. While I had originally adopted Coal, Dixie decided he had no use for a little brother, so he went to live happily with Lucy and Ed and his cat sister, Snow.

I closed the refrigerator door and turned to her. "It's not like we're driving out into the boondocks. There are places to stop and get snacks if we need them. I don't know why I need to pack a bag."

She chuckled. "It's better to be prepared. What if we broke down on the side of the road? What if Lilly got hungry while we were waiting for somebody to come and get us? You don't want her crying the whole time because she's hungry."

I nodded and grabbed the small canvas bag, throwing it over my shoulder. "You're right. It's better to be prepared." I picked Lilly up and settled her on my hip as we headed out the door. We were going to have so much fun today.

CHAPTER 2

"Hold still, Lilly," I said as I tried to dab baby sunscreen onto her pink cheeks. She wiggled around, moving her head from side to side to keep me from putting any on her.

Lucy chuckled. "She doesn't like that one bit, does she?"

I shook my head. "No, Sarah said she would give me a run for my money, and she wasn't kidding." It was hard to hit a moving target, and Lilly was determined to keep moving. "If the sun weren't shining so brightly, I would consider skipping the sunscreen." Lilly had gone from being a sweet baby to a toddler on a tear.

"Oh no, you can't do that. Even if it's cloudy, the

sun will still get through, and her skin is so pink she'll get a sunburn."

I sighed. "I know, I just always hated this. When the kids were little, I would make their father put their sunscreen on. They always held still for him."

She leaned against the car. "Isn't that just like a kid? Their father tells them to sit still, and they do it. If their mother says sit still, they take off running. I don't understand it."

"I saw a program on television one time that explained it. Kids react differently to a deeper, lower voice and that's why they're more inclined to do what their fathers tell them to do. I tried lowering my voice a few times, but my kids just ignored me." I put sunscreen on the tips of Lilly's ears and straightened up, picking her up and putting her on my hip. "Ready?"

Lucy nodded. "Ready and waiting," she said, carrying our baskets. I had gotten Lilly a little pink woven basket. She could have fun trying to fill it up with blueberries.

Easley Farms spanned nearly a hundred acres and was primarily planted in blueberries. A smaller portion of the farm was planted with tomatoes, zucchini, onions, and cucumbers, and there was a bog where they planted cranberries as well, but most people knew them for the wild blueberries. You could either come and pick your own or go to the farm stand and buy them already picked. I'll be honest and say most of the time, that was what I did, but there was no way I was going to skip out on a fun morning with my granddaughter.

We passed through the open gate and onto the farm. Earlier in the spring, they had planted strawberries and sold them at the farm stand. There was no strawberry picking for the public, but they were sweet and juicy, just the way you would expect fresh strawberries to be. We walked past the farm stand where people stood in line to buy their blueberries, and I shook my head, glancing at Lucy. "Look at those poor schmucks. They could be having a lovely family experience, taking the kids out into the field and picking their blueberries, but instead, they're buying them already picked."

She nodded. "Exactly. Bringing the kids to a place like this is the highlight of the summer. My parents brought us to the farms to pick blueberries every year, and we loved it. Okay, maybe I'm lying. We probably had other things we wanted to do since it was the end of summer, but I have fond memories of our family outings anyway."

I chuckled. "Sometimes when you're a kid, you miss out on fun things only because you want to do something else." I turned to look at Lilly on my hip. "I bet you're the best blueberry picker in all of Maine."

She didn't look at me, but she smiled as she took in the sights of the farm. I was sure she understood what I said.

"I bet it's a lot of work keeping these blueberries going," Lucy said as we walked the paved path that led through the fields of blueberry bushes. Half of the farm's blueberries were in a prune year, while the other half were ready to be picked. Each year, they alternated halves of the farm so they would always have plenty of blueberries ready for harvest.

After we had walked for a few minutes, I turned to Lucy. "What about these? Don't these blueberries look good?" I nodded at the nearby rows of bushes.

She squinted at the bushes as we walked. "No, let's walk on further. All the bushes that are closer to the fruit stand have been picked over. People are too lazy to walk to the end of the fields. The best fruit will be out there."

I nodded. "You've got a point. Everybody stops at the nearest bushes and strips them clean."

"What they don't know is that the sweeter berries are in the furthest fields," she said.

We walked along, and Lilly started squirming, begging to be let down. I held onto her for a few minutes, but then realized the struggle was in vain. There was no way I was going to win this one. "Lilly, I'm going to put you down, and I expect you to stay on this path." As soon as the soles of her shoes hit the pavement, she took off running.

"At least she listens well," Lucy chuckled.

I shot her a look. "For sure."

We started after Lilly at a trot, allowing her just enough space to feel like she was a big girl and was leading the way.

"It's a good thing we skipped our run earlier because we're going to get it in now," Lucy said as we trotted along.

I nodded. "The girl is a runner. It won't be long before she'll be joining us on our morning runs."

"That will be so much fun. I hope she likes coffee."

I laughed. "I guess we can get her hot cocoa instead of coffee. Our stop at the Cup and Bean

Coffee Shop after a run is almost obligatory at this point."

Lilly did a good job staying on the path, although she zigzagged from one side to the other. As long as she remained within my sight, I was fine with that.

"I'm starting to sweat," Lucy groaned as she wiped her brow with the back of her hand.

I nodded. "It's really warm out today."

We ran past fields of blueberry bushes, my canvas bag of snacks bouncing on my back as we trotted. I was going to have to drink something soon if we kept this up much longer, and I was glad we brought the bottled water. I pointed at the bushes. "What about those?"

Lucy turned to glance in the direction I was pointing. "There are more blueberries on these bushes than the other ones. Let's go a little bit further though."

I nodded, and we continued to follow Lilly. I glanced around at the field, noting that there wasn't anyone picking blueberries this far out. That was good. These were going to be untouched berries. Lilly suddenly slowed to a walk, shaking her head and muttering to herself. When Lucy and I caught up, her cheeks were bright pink. "It's a good thing we put sunscreen on, young lady."

She looked up at me and grinned as we kept walking.

"How about these?" Lucy said, nodding to the right.

"They look great." I took Lilly's hand and steered her over toward the bushes. "Now, Lilly, we're going to pick only the dark blueberries and put them in our baskets." I handed her the pink basket, which she took eagerly, and then I demonstrated by picking a ripe blueberry and dropping it into her basket. "Just like that."

She nodded and grabbed a blueberry, pulling it from the bush with exaggerated effort, and dropping it into the basket.

"Good girl," Lucy said, standing beside her and picking some of her own blueberries. "We'll have our baskets filled in no time."

I started picking berries for my own basket. They looked so plump that I couldn't help but pop one into my mouth. The fresh, slightly tart flavor burst in my mouth. "That is so good."

Lucy picked a berry, put it in her mouth, and nodded. "Delicious. I told you it was going to be worth the walk to get these."

Not to be outdone, Lilly grabbed a berry that was

still slightly green. Before I could warn her, she popped it into her mouth. She chewed, then spat it out, wiping her mouth with her chubby little fingers. "Uh uh." She shook her head.

"Oh no," I said. "Lilly, we've got to pick only the dark blueberries." I picked one for her and handed it to her. "It's okay. I promise it will taste good."

After a moment's consideration, she took the berry from me, put it in her mouth, chewed, and then nodded appreciatively before grabbing another one and eating it.

"There you go," I said, then went back to picking blueberries.

Lilly kept putting berries into her mouth instead of her basket. I should have seen that one coming.

"Don't eat too many of them, sweetie," Lucy warned as she filled her basket.

But once she had tasted the delectable fruit, she wasn't going to stop. I hadn't thought this through. "Let's put some in your basket," I encouraged, putting some blueberries into her basket for her.

She looked at the berries I had just put in there, reached into the basket, and then popped three of them into her mouth. A bit of blueberry juice puddled in the corners of her lips.

I groaned. "Lilly, you can't eat too many berries. They'll want to weigh you on the way out."

"They're not weighing me," Lucy said, popping two more blueberries into her mouth.

I chuckled. "We're going to get into trouble if we eat too many of them, but they sure are good." I placed a few more berries into my basket, and then Lilly suddenly bolted down the row of bushes mumbling something about 'boo berries'.

"Hey! Where are you going?" I put my basket on the ground and chased after her.

Lucy laughed. "You get the kid, I'll get the berries."

Lilly ran faster than I thought possible as she sprinted down the row of bushes. What were they feeding this kid? "Lilly, you get back here!" But instead of coming back, she just ran a little faster. I groaned.

Suddenly, Lilly darted through a gap between blueberry bushes, and I chased after her, barely squeezing through the place she had easily slipped through. "Lilly! Come back!"

"Do you need some help?" Lucy called.

"No, I've got her," I called over my shoulder. Lilly darted down another row of blueberry bushes.

"I mean it, young lady," I said, trying to sound

stern. But Lilly knew as well as I did that I was never going to be truly stern with her.

Lilly jogged to the left, and I followed, but when I reached the row, I swore she had just gone down. She wasn't there. I stood there, breathing hard and glancing around, trying to figure out where she had gone. "Lilly?"

I took a deep breath and listened, but there was only silence.

"Lilly!" I shouted. "Lilly!" I hurried down the row of bushes, then darted through a gap created by a missing bush and tripped, slamming into the ground. Stunned, it took me a moment before I realized what had happened. Lilly giggled somewhere nearby.

"I've got her!" Lucy called.

I got to my aching knees, brushed dirt off my skinned elbows and my cute little flip-flop T-shirt, and then got to my feet. Sandals were not made for running. I looked over my shoulder to see what I had tripped over and something white caught my eye. It took me a few seconds before I understood what I was seeing. It was a very large bone.

CHAPTER 3

inding a dead body on my granddaughter's first blueberry-picking excursion was the last thing I expected. We hadn't even gathered many blueberries in our basket by the time we found him or her. Baking a blueberry cheesecake would have to wait.

Lucy sat on one of the benches the farm had put out for customers to rest, her arms crossed in front of her. She wore a sleeveless blue and white top with denim shorts and looked perfectly miserable. "I can't believe this happened. How are we going to make blueberry cheesecake?"

I shook my head as I watched my husband, Alec, the lead detective with the local police department, taking pictures of the area where we had found the body. My son had driven out to the blueberry farm, picked Lilly up, and taken her home. Thankfully, she hadn't seen a thing. She was so intent on running down the rows of blueberry bushes that she hadn't noticed anything amiss in her surroundings. Most of the body had been beneath the bushes anyway, with just the leg sticking out that I had tripped over, and Lilly hadn't gone down that particular row. Not that she would have understood what she was looking at, but just the same, I had rather she didn't see it.

Several farm workers stood around, talking to one another, keeping an eye on Alec as he worked. As more police officers arrived, the look on their faces grew more grim.

I got up and headed over to where Alec was working and squatted down. "How's it going?"

He glanced at me, a bead of sweat running down his forehead, which he swiped away. "It's going all right, I guess. It looks like she's been in the ground for a while."

"She?"

"That's what it looks like to me." The edges of his dark hair grew wet with sweat as he worked. The day turned warmer than expected.

I nodded, glancing at the woman beneath the bushes. Her clothes were caked in dirt, and there wasn't much left of her other than a skeleton, with one leg bone sticking out from her pant leg. "I wonder how long she's been here?"

He shook his head. "The coroner will have to figure that out, but she's been exposed to the elements, so I'm guessing anywhere from a year or more. Could be three, but since they come through and cultivate these bushes every other year, I can't imagine why no one saw her if she was here longer."

I squinted up at the sun and looked at him again. "Last spring we got an awful lot of rain, and we had that bad rainstorm a few weeks ago. Maybe she wasn't buried very deep, and the rain washed the dirt away, exposing her."

He nodded as he continued taking pictures. "I think that's probably what happened."

I shook my head. I felt bad for whoever this woman was, and I wondered how she had ended up beneath the blueberry bushes.

"Does she have any ID on her?" Lucy asked from behind me. I glanced over my shoulder, startled, as I hadn't heard her approach.

Alec looked up at her. "I haven't found any ID. We

might find something when we move her, though. I've called the coroner, and he should be here soon."

I nodded. "A lot of the farm workers are gathering."

Alec looked over his shoulder and back to the body. "A dead body brings a lot of interest."

"I wonder if it's because one of them is the killer," I said. Lucy and I had gone on fact-finding missions in the past when there was a murder, and my mind was always searching for answers. I couldn't help but wonder if one of these farm workers was responsible for this woman's death. It seemed plausible.

"It's possible," Alec echoed my thoughts.

"Alec, what do you want me to do?" Yancey Tucker, one of the other officers, asked as he approached.

He looked up at him. "See if you can help me find any clues around here."

Yancey then glanced at Lucy and me. "Ladies."

"Hello, Yancey," I said. "How are you?"

"Fancy meeting you here, Yancey," Lucy said.

He smiled. "Yeah, who would've thought it? I'm doing okay, Allie."

As Yancey began searching the nearby area for clues, I heard the door of a vehicle slam. I looked up to see an old truck parked near the edge of the blue-berry bushes. Grace Easley, one of the owners of this family farm hurried down the path, almost at a run. She wore a purple flowered dress that had a white background and brown sandals. Her short, curly brown hair bobbed with each step.

When she had almost reached us, an officer stood in her path to prevent her from getting close enough to see the body, and another quickly joined him.

"Is it my daughter? Is that Lainey?" she asked, standing on tiptoe and breathing hard as she looked in Alec's direction.

Alec looked at Lucy and me, then stood up and headed over to where the Grace was trying to push past the two officers.

"I'm Detective Alec Blanchard. Who did you ask about?" Alec asked, extending his hand as he intro-duced himself.

The woman looked down at his open hand and then back up at him. "Lainey. Easley. My daughter. She's missing." She took a breath. "Is it her? Did you find her body?"

Lucy and I looked at each other and then back at Grace. I hadn't heard that her daughter was missing, and my heart went out to her.

"How long has your daughter been missing?" Alec asked. "Have you filed a police report?"

She hesitated and ran a hand through her hair. "No, we haven't filed a missing persons report. Can I see her? I need to know if that's my daughter."

Alec eyed her. "What do you mean you didn't file a missing persons report? If your daughter has been missing, why wouldn't you file a report?"

The woman took a deep breath again and exhaled. "Well, I don't actually know that she's missing, exactly. It's just that I haven't heard from her for a while, and I've been worried about her. And now that there's a body found here on the blueberry farm, of course my mind goes to that."

She looked at me and Lucy. "Allie, is it her? Is it Lainey?"

I didn't know how to answer her at first, and when I opened my mouth to say something, I looked at Alec, who gave me a stern look. He turned back to her. "What do you mean you haven't heard from her? How long has it been? And why would you not be in contact with her?" Alec pulled a small notebook from his pocket.

She shook her head. "Our relationship with Lainey has been difficult. Mine and my husband's and my sons, I mean. Lainey has always been a free spirit; you can't tell her anything. She lives life on her terms, and that never sat well with her father. She moved out of the house about five years ago, and even though our relationship was difficult, we still kept in touch. Then she moved to Oregon about two years ago." She wrung her hands in front of herself, leaning past Alec to see if she could catch a glimpse of the body. It wouldn't matter if she saw the body anyway; there was no way anyone was going to be able to ID the woman visually.

"And when was the last time you spoke to her?" Alec asked.

Grace sighed. "I don't know. I guess it was almost two years ago. A year and a half. She was supposed to come home and spend Christmas with us the year before last, but she never showed up. I tried calling her, but she didn't answer." She looked away, shaking her head. "Why didn't I call the police then? I should have, but this wasn't unusual behavior for her. Sometimes we didn't talk for months." She turned back, looking perplexed now.

Another pickup drove up and parked behind the one Grace had been driving, and her husband, Frank Easley, got out and stormed down the narrow path.

"What's going on here?" he demanded. "Grace? What's going on?" Frank Easley was a tall, stout man with blond hair and a ruddy complexion.

Grace turned to him, shaking her head. "Oh, Frank, they found the body of a woman here in the blueberry field. It's Lainey. I just know it."

Frank's eyes widened as he came to a stop. He shook his head. "No, that's not true. Why would she be here? She wouldn't be out here in these blueberry fields. You know how she was; she hated the blueberry farm."

I glanced behind them as the other farmworkers began to huddle together. They were whispering to one another, and it made me wonder what was being said.

Alec introduced himself to Frank. "When was the last time you saw your daughter, Mr. Easley?"

Frank drew up to his full height of well over six feet and shook his head. "I don't know. The girl didn't want anything to do with me, and it's been a couple of years or more. She never called me, she never wanted to talk to me. I don't have any idea when it was I last spoke to her. She didn't show up for Christmas year before last."

Grace shook her head, tears springing to her eyes.

"It's true she had a lot of issues with her father, but like I said, she was supposed to be here for Christmas a year and a half ago, and she never showed up."

"I'm sure she just had a fit about something and didn't want to make the trip," Frank said bitterly. "That's the way she was. You never knew what she was going to do, and I'm sure somebody did or said something that made her angry. She just decided not to show up. If there's a body under those bushes, then it has to be someone else. Why do you think that's my daughter over there?"

Alec shook his head. "We don't know that it's her. Grace here insisted that it was, but we haven't found any identification yet. It's going to take us a while to work the crime scene and see what else we can find."

"Well, why do you think it's a crime scene?" Frank asked. "Did you see something that made you think it's a crime scene? Do you think somebody murdered Lainey?"

"To be honest, I don't know at this point if it's a crime scene, but we're going to treat it as if it is one until we know for sure," Alec answered. "Do you have any idea why she would be out here in the blueberry field and why she might suddenly die if she wasn't murdered? Assuming it's your daughter."

Grace hesitated and then shook her head. "I guess I don't know. But she wouldn't be out here on her own. Like Frank said, she hated the blueberry farm and didn't want anything to do with it."

A third truck approached and parked behind Frank's truck, and their son Bryce got out of it and trotted down the path. It was getting to be a regular family reunion, and I wondered if Lainey really was the woman beneath that blueberry bush. Bryce's eyes widened. "What's going on here, Dad? Mom?" He glanced at Alec and the other officers.

"They found a dead woman beneath the blueberry bushes," Grace said, gasping. "I just know it's Lainey. It has to be Lainey."

Bryce's eyes widened and he shook his head. "What? What are you talking about? Why would Lainey be dead out here underneath a blueberry bush? She's not dead." He looked at Alec for reassurance. "Right?"

"We don't know for sure until we get some identification on the body," Alec said. "I'm going to need to speak to all three of you and get your statements."

I glanced at Lucy, and she shook her head at me. "So sad," she whispered.

I leaned my head toward her. "It's awful. I hope it's not their daughter beneath that blueberry bush."

We watched as Alec spoke with the family and then went and sat on the bench, waiting until Alec dismissed us. We had told him what we saw, which wasn't much, but I didn't know if he needed anything else from us. I glanced at the farmworkers who were still gathered in a circle discussing the day's events and wondered if they knew what happened to the woman beneath the blueberry bush.

CHAPTER 4

I sat in the recliner with an old black-and-white movie on the television, which I was ignoring while keeping one eye on the clock over the mantle. The first days of an investigation were busy ones, and I didn't expect Alec to be home early. It was now almost nine o'clock in the evening. Dixie sat in my lap as I absentmindedly stroked his back. I was grateful Lilly had been too preoccupied running down the rows of blueberry bushes to have seen what I saw. Not that she would have understood if she had seen it, of course, but I felt better knowing she hadn't.

The woman in the blueberry field had been dead for a while. If it was Frank and Grace Easley's daughter, what was she doing out there? Especially if she hated the farm, as her father said. My mind ran through various scenarios, but until we had details, there wasn't much we could know.

I took a sip from my glass of sweet tea that sat on the end table. The ice had melted long ago, and I sighed. "Dixie, if Alec isn't home soon, we'll have to go to bed without him." Dixie flicked one ear back toward me but didn't move. I had no intention of going to bed early, of course, because I wanted to hear everything he had found out when he got home.

I took a deep breath when I heard the keys in the front door lock. "Looks like he's home." I set Dixie on the ottoman and hurried to the front door.

The door swung open and I could tell by the look in his eyes he was tired. "Well, good evening."

I smiled. "Good evening yourself. How are you doing?" I held my arms out to him, and he stepped into my embrace.

He kissed me, then looked at me. "I'm doing great. Well, maybe not great since I've got another murder on my hands, but I'm doing as well as I can be. And I'm starving."

I nodded. "I made salmon. I'll warm some up for you."

We headed to the kitchen with his arm wrapped around my waist. "I love salmon."

"I know," I said. "That's why I made it. Now tell me everything. Don't leave anything out."

He sat down at the kitchen table and groaned. "I'm beat."

"I bet you are," I said, going to the refrigerator and removing the plate of food I had made for him: grilled salmon, asparagus, and a baked potato. If I hadn't been starving earlier, I would have waited to eat dinner with him, but I never knew when he would get home on the first day of an investigation. I popped the plate into the microwave and turned it on, then went and grabbed two glasses and filled them with ice and sweet tea.

"I pulled a few strings and got Lainey Easley's dental records from her dentist."

I looked at him with one eyebrow raised as I brought the glasses of iced tea over and set them on the table. "Then it really is Frank and Grace's daughter?"

He nodded and took a long sip of his tea, then he set the glass on the table. "Yes, I figured we might as well start with the most obvious person, and that was their missing daughter. Her dentist sent us her most recent X-rays within a few minutes, and I sent them over to the medical examiner. It didn't take long for him to identify her."

I went to the microwave to check on his food and when it was finished heating, I brought it back to the table for him and set it in front of him. "That's a shame. How old was she?"

"Twenty-four. It is a shame. Aren't you going to eat something?"

I sat down across from him and shook my head. "No, I already ate." I knew it didn't take long to identify a body through dental records, but even this was fast. "I'm glad they were able to ID her so quickly. Any idea how she died?"

He shook his head. "No, there weren't any obvious signs. The medical examiner said she had been in the ground for a while."

I gazed at him, puzzled. "Then why was she out of the ground when we found her? And why hadn't anybody else found her before now?"

He cut into his salmon with the side of his fork. "Must have been all that rain we got this spring. I think it washed her out of the grave."

"It must have been a shallow grave," I said.

He nodded. "And as far as why nobody had found

her body, it was because the three of you had gone beyond the blueberry field customers were supposed to go to pick. The bushes in the back in that area were for the farm workers to pick blueberries to sell in the stand. Most of them weren't ripe, so the field hadn't been worked yet."

"Well, we didn't see that it was marked anywhere. We weren't trespassing."

He chuckled. "I think you were. Frank said most customers stick to the closer fields. That field was due to be harvested in the next week or two." He ate the piece of salmon on his fork and nodded appreciatively. "This is good."

I nodded. "Thanks. I've been dying to try out that recipe for honey-ginger sauce I saw online a few weeks ago."

"Well, this recipe is a keeper," he said. "I couldn't find any personal effects other than her clothes, which were still in the shallow grave. The leg bone you tripped over became detached, and the rain most likely washed it out of the grave." He looked up at me. "Oh, and there was a key in the pocket of her jeans."

I shook my head. "What kind of key? House key?"

He shook his head. "No, it looks smaller than that. We're not sure what it goes to yet."

"Anything else? Her purse wasn't there?" I needed details if I was going to hunt for Lainey's killer.

"No, we haven't been able to find her purse. We're going to go back tomorrow and do some more digging when it's daylight. It's possible it was discarded underneath one of the bushes."

I took a sip of my iced tea, thinking this over. "Any chance she could have just died back there and nobody knew? Maybe she had some kind of heart issue."

"It's possible." He took another bite of his salmon and nodded appreciatively.

"But nobody had any idea she was there all this time." That was the part that bothered me the most.

He shook his head. "No, last year was a prune year for the blueberries in that field, and this is the year they're harvested. The workers at the farm have been back in that area checking on the bushes and making sure the water lines are in working order. But it's been several weeks since anyone has been back there."

I nodded. "The spring rains probably softened the ground really well, and the last storm a few weeks ago washed her leg out." I shuddered. "How awful. I'm glad her family members weren't the ones who found her."

He scooped some of his baked potato onto his fork and nodded. "Me too."

"Where did Frank and Grace think their daughter was all this time? And how long has she been missing?"

"She's been estranged from the family for several years. They were happy when she said she would come for Christmas the year before last, but she never showed up. They figured she had gotten angry about something and decided not to come. According to Grace, Lainey has always been moody, and it only increased the older she got."

"When was the last time they saw her?" I felt sorry for the Easleys. It must have been difficult having this strain on their relationships.

"A few years ago. She had been in and out of the house since she turned eighteen, and when she was twenty, she moved into an apartment here in town but refused to see them. Then, October before last, she moved to Oregon. At first, they claimed she got on the airplane to come back to Maine, but when I pressed them, they said all they knew was that she said that's what she was going to do on December twenty-first. They all assumed she got on the plane."

I shook my head. "So they weren't even sure she

had made it back to town until now? That's sad that they didn't get to see their daughter one more time before she died. Nobody saw her here in Maine that December?"

"They assumed she stayed with friends when she got here, but they didn't know who all of her friends were. None of the family saw her, but I'm going to be talking to some of her friends who still live here in town and see if they saw her."

I sighed and took a sip of my sweet tea. "I guess she must have been out in those blueberries for the past year and a half then unless somebody had her body and brought her out to the farm. That could be why nobody spotted her. If she had recently been placed in a shallow grave, then it wouldn't have taken much for the rainstorm to wash her out. But then that means somebody has held onto that body for a while, and where would they put it?"

He chuckled. "That would be tricky. I'm betting the body has been out there all this time and nobody came across it."

"You're probably right. The poor thing." I yawned. It was still early, but the excitement of the day had worn me out.

His brow furrowed. "Don't get started with that

yawning. You'll have me doing it," he said as he put a forkful of asparagus into his mouth.

I smiled. "I'll ask around and see if I can find out if anybody saw Lainey when she got to town. She may have visited with her friends and planned to go to see her family on Christmas morning, but she was killed first. That would have given her a few days to be here in town, and somebody had to have seen her if she wasn't killed right away."

I didn't know exactly when Lainey had been murdered, but I had a sneaking suspicion that since she was having troubles with her family, she wasn't going to spend any extra time with them other than Christmas day. She would have flown out here to Maine, hung out with her friends, and then planned on making the obligatory visit on Christmas morning.

CHAPTER 5

*T*he following morning, Lucy and I went for a run. When we finished, we headed over to the Cup and Bean coffee shop. There's nothing like an iced coffee after a morning run to set the tone for the rest of the day. And then there were their freshly baked muffins and scones that were like the cherry on top of an ice cream sundae.

"I'm so glad Lilly didn't see anything yesterday," Lucy said, lowering her voice as I paid for our coffee and muffins. I had gone with the iced raspberry mocha, and Lucy had chosen an iced caramel latte. Both of our muffins were chocolate chip.

I nodded. "Me too." We picked up our order and headed over to Mr. Winters's table. Mr. Winters was an elderly man who had become our friend. At first, it was because he was good at getting information out of people when we were unofficially working a case, but later it was because he was a wonderful person.

He looked up at us and nodded. "Ladies."

"Good morning, Mr. Winters," Lucy said as we sat down across from him. "It's a beautiful day, isn't it?"

He nodded again and folded over his newspaper. "I heard a rumor around town, by the way. There was a murder." He leaned over the table. "I bet you two have information about it."

I was surprised the news had traveled so fast, but maybe I shouldn't have been. Sandy Harbor was a small town and people liked to talk. "Who did you hear it from?" I asked.

"Grant Eggleston. I went to the barbershop first thing this morning and got a trim. Didn't you notice?" He tipped his head toward us so we could have a look.

I eyed his thinning white hair. "Well, yes, now that you mention it, I do see you've gotten a haircut. It looks very nice."

He smiled. "So who is it? What happened? Don't hold back on me."

I reached beneath the table and patted his little gray poodle, Sadie. She wagged her tail, thumping it against the floor, and put her cold nose against my bare leg. I leaned forward. "Lainey Easley. Did you know her?"

His eyes widened slightly. "Well, I didn't know her so well, but I've known the Easleys for years. Even knew Lainey's grandparents, Ida and Clem Easley. They bought that farm years ago and worked it all their lives. Or almost all their lives. What a shame. I had no idea. I'll have to stop by and see Frank and Grace."

I nodded somberly. "Yes, it's really sad. Apparently, Lainey had been estranged from them for a while. How well do you know the Easleys?"

He shrugged. "I've been to a handful of barbecues at their house, but it's been years since that happened. Before Clem passed away. Whenever I see Frank or Grace around town, we always stop to talk. Sure is a shame."

"It really is," Lucy said. "It looks like Lainey was out there in the field for a while."

I gave her a look. We couldn't give out too much information yet.

He looked at her, one eyebrow raised. "Is that so? That's strange. Where did they think she was while she was missing?"

"She was supposed to come home for Christmas the year before last, but she never made it," I said. "With them being estranged, they just thought she had changed her mind and hadn't told them she wouldn't be coming."

He thought about this for a moment. "I know that Frank has quite the temper. Maybe that's why she was estranged."

"Really?" I said, taking this in. "Do you think he abused her?"

He shook his head. "Frank isn't the type. But I know he had a temper. Jamison Brown used to work for him a few years back, and he got tired of him yelling all the time, so he quit. I asked him if he did that to everyone who worked for him at the farm, and he said yes. I think it's just part of his personality."

"That's a terrible personality trait to have," Lucy said, taking a sip of her iced coffee. "You'll chase people off that way, and maybe that's what he did to his daughter."

"But they're good people," Mr. Winters defended. "Maybe some people are too sensitive and take him the wrong way. I don't think he means to be unkind." He took a sip of his black coffee.

I was about to say something else when Ellen

Allen approached our table. For a second, I didn't recognize her without her green hair; it was dark brown now, and the multiple piercings she normally had in her nose were missing. It looked like Ellen was making a change.

She narrowed her eyes at me. "Allie, what's going on? Somebody murdered my cousin, and I want to know who did it. Has your husband found the killer?"

"Lainey Easley was your cousin?" I asked. I had no idea the Easleys were related to Ellen Allen. Ellen was what you might call a problematic person. Lucy had worked with her years ago at the florist shop, but Ellen had been fired for stealing. She swore she hadn't taken anything, but the former owner of the florist shop said she had taken money from the cash register. Later, she admitted that she had borrowed the money to buy medicine for her mother. While it was noble that she wanted to make sure her mother got her medicine, it was still stealing.

She nodded. "Yes, she was my cousin, and we were close. I just can't believe anyone would murder her. Does your husband know who did it yet?"

I shook my head. "Not yet, but he's working diligently on the case. When was the last time you saw Lainey?"

She licked her bottom lip. Her mascara was smudged beneath her eyes, making her look older than her thirty or so years. "It's been about two years ago. She and her dad got into a fight, and she left to go to Oregon. But we still kept in contact. We texted and emailed each other all the time. When she quit contacting me a little over a year and a half ago, I couldn't understand it. Now I guess I know. Your husband needs to find her killer. Now."

I nodded. "As I said, he's doing everything he can to find her killer. Do you have any idea what might have happened? Did you see her when she came to town the December before last?"

She shook her head. "No, I didn't see her when she came to town. Whoever killed her must have done it as soon as she got here. Can you believe it? Somebody killed her right before Christmas." She sighed, putting her hands on her hips. Ellen was tall, probably close to six feet, and wore a thin fuchsia-colored sweater and Capri jeans that were far too short for her tall build.

"It seems even more cruel when someone is killed before Christmas," I agreed. It always made me sad when somebody got killed on a major holiday. Their family who had been left behind, would always dread that holiday when it came around each year.

"Well, let me tell you something," she said, her voice rising. "She broke up with her boyfriend that September. Jim Martin. He was a real jerk. She told me he threatened her because he thought she was looking at another guy. But I know my cousin, and she would never do something like that."

"Oh?" Lucy said. "She initiated the breakup?"

She glared at Lucy, and for a moment, I thought she wouldn't answer her, but then she nodded, her short brown hair bobbing with the motion. "Yes, she's the one who broke up with him. She said he kept calling her after that, begging her to come back to him, and each time she told him no, he got angry. I'm putting my money on him as the killer."

"Have you talked to Alec?" I asked.

She shook her head. "No, I haven't talked to Alec. He didn't come around asking to talk to me."

"Maybe he didn't know he needed to ask you about the murder," Lucy said. "But if you have information, and this sounds like information that might be helpful, go and talk to him."

I almost rolled my eyes. "Yes, Ellen, he's not a mind reader. You've got to call him and let him know you have information that might be important to the case. He wants to find your cousin's killer as much as you want them found."

"Jim Martin," Mr. Winters suddenly spoke up. "He's the grandson of a friend of mine. My friend doesn't have much positive to say about his grandson. Other than he's lazy and doesn't want to work, and he can't abide by that."

I turned to him. "Did he ever say if his grandson was violent?"

He thought for a moment, then shook his head. "No, I don't recall him ever saying that, but maybe I've forgotten it."

Ellen sighed and rolled her eyes. "All I know is that he killed my cousin, and I want your husband to arrest him, Allie. I hope he gets the death penalty. He deserves it."

"There's no death penalty in Maine anymore," I pointed out.

She snorted. "Oh, of course not. There are too many soft people around here." She crossed her arms in front of herself. "Murderers need to get the death penalty. It's only right."

I smiled. "I know Alec is going to do everything he can to find your cousin's killer and arrest them.

Maybe they'll get life in prison."

She sighed again. "I guess if that's the most they can do, we'll have to settle for it." Her bottom lip started trembling. "Honestly, Lainey was a sweetheart. She had a heart of gold, and she was too good to people. People like to take advantage of people like that, you know. I told her she should have broken up with Jim months earlier. She had no business even going out with him. He's just an awful person."

"So you think he killed her just because she wouldn't take him back?" Lucy asked, taking another sip of her iced coffee.

She hesitated. "Sure, I think that must have been the reason. There isn't any other reason I can think of." She glanced over her shoulder, then turned back. "I have to get going. I've got to get to work. Have your husband call me, and I'll tell him all I know about Jim."

"Ellen, why don't you call him and tell him you have something to say about the case?" I asked. I wasn't anybody's secretary, and certainly not Ellen Allen's.

She eyed me. "Sure, I guess I gotta do everything, don't I? I'll call your husband, all right. But he better get Jim Martin arrested or else." She spun and headed to the front door, shoving it open roughly when she got to it.

"She has to do everything," Lucy mocked, turning to me.

I shook my head. "That Ellen Allen has always been kind of a jerk."

"You don't have to tell me. I know all about it."

CHAPTER 6

I knew Jim Martin well enough to say hello whenever I saw him around town, and when I saw him duck into the ice cream shop as I was going to get stamps at the post office, I changed directions and followed him into the shop.

There was a short line at the counter, and I got into it behind him. "Hi Jim, how have you been?"

He glanced over his shoulder and smiled when he realized who was speaking to him. "Oh, Allie. I've been good. How are you?"

I smiled. "I've had a hankering for some praline ice cream, and since it's a warm day, I decided it was the perfect time to stop by for some. I haven't seen you around town for a while." Jim had been in Thad's class and had been a sweet, shy boy.

He shook his head and half-turned toward me. "I got a job as a janitor at the elementary school, and that keeps me busy these days. When I worked at the hardware store, my schedule varied, but now I work the same one every day."

I nodded. "Good for you. Those jobs at the school are always good ones. How do you like it?"

He shrugged. "I guess cleaning toilets isn't my favorite thing to do, but I can deal with it. I get to spend a lot of time by myself and I listen to podcasts while I work." Jim was tall and thin with sandy hair.

"Oh, that's a plus," I said. "I love listening to a good podcast, especially the true crime ones. Do you ever listen to true crime podcasts?"

He nodded. "Oh sure, I enjoy listening to those. I always try to figure out who the killer is before they get to the end. I've gotten pretty good at it, too."

Ah ha. "It is a lot of fun trying to figure out the mystery, isn't it? Unfortunately, somebody had to die for there to be a mystery to begin with, though. I'm not crazy about that, but that can't be helped, I guess. Did you hear there was a murder at the Easley's blueberry farm?"

His eyes widened for a moment, then he nodded. "Yeah, I heard it was Lainey Easley. I was surprised when I heard about it."

"Were you? I guess I was surprised too. Did you know Lainey?"

He nodded, glancing at the short line in front of us. "Yeah, I knew her. We dated for seven or eight months the year she left for Oregon. Honestly, I can't imagine who would want to kill her like that. She was a sweet girl."

"Oh, my goodness, I'm so sorry," I said. "I didn't realize the two of you dated. If you were together when she disappeared, it had to have been heart-breaking to hear she was missing, wasn't it? And now that she's dead?" I shook my head sadly. "I'm so sorry."

He scooted up in the line as it moved. "Yeah, well, like I said, we had broken up before she disappeared. I wasn't even aware she had disappeared for a while until a friend of mine mentioned she didn't come home for Christmas like she had planned. But by that time, I had moved on with my life. I'm married now." He held up his hand to show me a gold band.

"Oh Jim, congratulations! I'm so happy for you. Who did you marry?"

"Taylor Jenkins. She's the sweetest girl I ever

dated, and I knew I couldn't let her get away." The grin on his face said he was happy as a clam.

"I know Taylor, and you're right. She is a sweet girl. Good for you, and good for her. I'm so happy to hear you got married."

He nodded, looking bashful now. "Yeah, I think this is the happiest I've ever been. We've only been married for two months, but it's the best decision I ever made."

I nodded, keeping my eye on his face as he spoke. "Must have been a shock when you heard that Lainey's body was found out at the blueberry farm, especially since you were close once. I just can't imagine who could have done that to her. You don't have any idea, do you?"

He hesitated before answering. "No, I guess I don't have any idea who might have wanted to kill her. And you're right. It was a shock to hear her body had been found. I never thought somebody would do that to her. I kind of wonder if maybe she wasn't murdered."

"What do you mean?" We moved up in line again.

He shook his head and scooted up a few more inches, creating a bigger gap between us before answering. "I don't know. It's just weird, is all. But I thought maybe she was out in one of the blueberry fields and she had an accident of some kind and couldn't get back to the house. Maybe she broke a leg and maybe it was snowing at the time. If she's been out in that field all this time, I think it would be hard to tell exactly what happened to her."

It seemed like Jim was really stretching to come up with an alternative to the murder scenario we were pretty certain had happened, and it made me wonder about him. "I don't know. I hadn't thought of that. My husband is working on the case, and he never mentioned anything like that. But forensics is a science, and I'm sure they can tell exactly what happened to her."

He looked at me again, and if I wasn't mistaken, his face went pale. "Your husband is working on the case?"

I nodded. "Yes, didn't you know I was married to a police detective?"

He shook his head slowly, looking surprised. "I guess I didn't know that. You must know a lot about the case, then."

I smiled. I thought everybody in town knew I was married to a police detective. "Oh no, Alec—that's my husband—can only tell me certain things about the cases he's working on. He doesn't want information to get out, you know. I told him he needs to tell me everything so I can help him solve the case, but he disagrees." I laughed. "But as I said, I enjoy those true crime podcasts, and every time Alec has a fresh case, I try to think about who the perpetrator might be."

He smiled and glanced away for a moment. "Well, I don't know who would have killed her, but I know that her father was a real jerk. He had a nasty temper, and she hated him."

"Hated? That's a strong word. Is that what she said?" I held my breath, hoping he knew something important.

He nodded as we moved up to the front counter. He turned away and ordered two scoops of Rocky Road ice cream on a sugar cone, then turned back to me. "Yeah, that's the word she used. At first, I thought she was just complaining to complain, but then she told me he was terrible to her and her brothers when they were kids. If they did something wrong, he would make them go out to the farm and work long hours as punishment."

"What do you mean?" I asked.

"You know, hoeing weeds, planting, or doing any manual labor he could think of. And he made them work all day long from sunup to sundown." He pulled his wallet out of his back pocket to pay for his ice cream. "Didn't let them have breaks, either."

I was stunned to hear this. Was Frank Easley that mean and vindictive? I hadn't heard anything negative about him other than what Ellen Allen had said. "That's an awful thing for a parent to do."

He thanked the woman behind the counter and turned to me, holding his ice cream cone. "Yeah, that's what I thought. Well, I better get going. I've got to pick up a few things at the grocery store before I go home."

"It was good talking to you, Jim. Tell Taylor I said congratulations, and have a good day."

"Thanks, you too," he said and headed out.

I stepped up to the counter and glanced at the menu board. "I think I'm going to get a scoop of praline ice cream in a cup, please."

The woman nodded and grabbed an ice cream scoop. "Coming right up." She glanced at me as she picked up a paper cup. "I heard about them finding a body out at the blueberry farm. Sure is a shame."

I smiled, glancing at the name tag on her apron. Gwen. She looked to be in her late sixties or early seventies. "It was just awful to hear about it. Did you know her?"

She hesitated, then shook her head. "I didn't know her, but her mother comes in here once or twice a week during the summer. We usually chat for a few minutes, and I enjoy going out to the farm to pick my own blueberries. There's nothing like farm-fresh produce."

"No, there certainly isn't. They have the best produce around." Did Gwen have something to say about the murder, I wondered?

She scooped a large scoop of ice cream and placed it into the cup. "It's a terrible shame what happened to that girl. I feel bad for her mother. The young man you were speaking to a minute ago isn't wrong about her father's temper. He had a full-on fit one day when I was at the fruit stand, picking up some cucumbers and blueberries. It was last year sometime, and I don't know what the fuss was about, but he was yelling at her."

"Lainey?"

She shook her head. "No, her mother. Grace. She ignored him, but I think it was because she was embarrassed and didn't want to provoke him further."

"That's awful that he did that in front of customers," I said. I was beginning to see another side of Frank that I didn't know existed.

She nodded. "It was awful. I felt so sorry for Grace, but I've never brought it up to her. I don't want to embarrass her."

I paid for my ice cream. If Frank was punishing his children by making them work on the farm for long hours at a time, I could see why Lainey wanted to get away from him and the farm. And I wondered if his anger finally got the best of him.

CHAPTER 7

$\mathcal{T}$he following morning, Lucy and I stopped by the blueberry farm to pick up more blueberries. I say "pick up" because we were just going to buy them at the farm stand instead of going out to pick them. I couldn't get Lainey Easley's murder out of my mind, and I wanted to see if I could speak to her mother, Grace.

The previous evening, I baked a chocolate cake to take to the family. "I can smell this cake through the bakery box," Lucy said, sighing. "It smells so good."

I smiled. "I think it turned out well. I added sour cream to make it more moist."

"Oh," she said, drawing out the word. "That

sounds so good. I love a good sour cream chocolate cake."

We got out of the car and headed up to the farmhouse. It was a big, two-story white clapboard house with a wraparound porch. "I can just imagine spending evenings rocking on that porch." My mother had a gorgeous porch like this one and I missed those summer evenings spent sitting out there and visiting with the neighbors.

Lucy nodded as she carried the cake. "Me too. I wish our house had a big porch like that."

"I wish I had a farm."

She turned to me as we walked. "Really? You'd like to live on a farm?"

I nodded. "Sure, wouldn't you? There's something about plants growing in the fields that makes me feel like all is right with the world. We could have a few animals, maybe some chickens and a goat. It would be a lot of fun, and Lilly would really enjoy herself."

"Alec doesn't strike me as the farmer type," she said with a chuckle. "And you do have a little bit of land with your house. Weren't you going to get Lilly a pony?"

"Yes, I intend to get Lilly a pony. Alec is fine with it, but I don't see him helping much with taking care of it. That's going to be all on me, I think." She was right. Alec wasn't the farmer type. It didn't matter, though, it wasn't like I wanted to buy a bunch of livestock or anything, but I intended to get that pony for Lilly when she was older.

We climbed the six stairs to the front porch, and I knocked on the door. It took several minutes before Grace answered it.

She smiled sadly at us. "Good morning, Allie, Lucy."

"Grace, we just stopped by to tell you how sorry we are for your loss," I said.

"Yes, we're so sorry," Lucy echoed.

She nodded. "I certainly appreciate that. It's kind of you to think of us."

"Grace, I baked a sour cream chocolate cake for you and your family," I said.

Her puffy and swollen eyes widened. "Oh, that's so sweet of you. Thank you, Allie. Would you ladies like to come in?"

"We'd love to," I said, as she pushed open the old-fashioned screen door so we could enter the house.

"Chocolate was Lainey's favorite," she said with a hitch in her voice as we followed her into the bright and airy living room. The hardwood floors gleamed,

61

and the overstuffed leather furniture was inviting. "I swear, that girl could eat chocolate for every meal of every day." She chuckled.

"That's a girl after my own heart," Lucy said as we sat down on the couch where she indicated. She set the chocolate cake on the coffee table between us.

Grace sat on the loveseat across from us and crossed her legs. "She was something else. A wild child from the beginning. Nothing could keep her down or hold her back, and I used to think about how I wouldn't know what I would do without her. I guess I'm going to find out now." Tears sprang to her eyes, and she dabbed at them with a crumpled tissue.

"I'm so sorry, Grace," I said. It broke my heart to see her this way.

She nodded. "Thank you. I appreciate it."

We all looked up as we heard boots on the hardwood floor headed in our direction. In a moment, her husband entered the living room. He hesitated, surprised to see us.

"Honey, Lucy and Allie have come to give their condolences. Allie baked us a sour cream chocolate cake, too," Grace explained.

Frank gave us a curt nod and came to sit down

next to his wife. "Does your husband have any idea who killed our daughter yet?"

"He's working very hard on the case," I assured them. "Hopefully, he'll have a breakthrough soon. Can I ask you both a question? You said she was supposed to come home for a Christmas visit. Did you not have any contact with her before this?"

"We made the arrangements for her flight on December twenty-first, but she never showed up," Grace said. "We didn't talk much other than about the trip."

"Did you check with the airlines to see if she ever got on the plane?" Lucy asked.

Grace glanced at her husband before answering. "No, because like I said, Lainey was a free spirit, and we had been having trouble with her for years. She moved off the farm when she was twenty and into her own apartment, and then she decided to leave the state just out of the blue."

Frank snorted. "An apartment that I paid for."

This wasn't the first time I sensed that Frank was resentful of his daughter. "Did she have a job?" I asked.

He snorted again. "I guess you could call it a job. She worked part-time at the movie theater. I had her doing a little bit of bookwork for the farm, but she rarely showed up to do it and rarely did it correctly."

"Usually, I handle most of the books for the farm," Grace said. "We wanted her to feel like she was a part of the farm though, so we had her do some of the work, but I'm afraid, as Frank said, she wasn't very reliable."

"Sometimes when people are young, they take a while to get their footing and to become good employees," I said. I didn't know what Lainey's problem was, but I could see where her behavior would cause resentment from her parents.

"Yes, I'm sure she would have gotten things straightened out eventually," Grace said, glancing sideways at her husband.

"If you don't mind my asking, do you have any idea who might have wanted to harm her?" I almost didn't want to ask it with Frank sitting there. It was easier to talk to Grace without him around.

"If you ask me, it was her boyfriend, Jim. The two of them broke up in the fall before she disappeared," he said. "He made Lainey miserable and she was always crying about things he had done."

"I don't think it would have been Jim," Grace said,

shaking her head. "The two were only casually dating. Why would he kill her if they weren't that serious?"

"Why do you think he might have done it?" I asked Frank.

He shook his head. "I don't know. It just seemed like it had to be somebody close to her. And I never liked him. He was immature."

"Jim was always polite when he was with her and when he was around us," Grace insisted. "I told this to Alec. I don't think he could have done anything to her, but I don't know who else would have done it either."

"I agree with you, Frank. It was probably somebody close to her," Lucy said. "Sometimes relationships can turn sour."

"You don't have to tell me that," he scowled. "I don't know what she would have been doing out in that blueberry field to begin with. Like I said, she hated the farm. We were surprised when she agreed and said she was coming home for Christmas. I figured she would pass on it, but maybe she thought she wouldn't get any Christmas presents if she didn't drop in. When she didn't show up, I wasn't surprised."

"Oh, Frank," Grace said, admonishing him. "Lainey just had some problems, that's all. She loved us all, and I know she wasn't trying to hurt us. There's a small part of me that is glad that she did try to show up for Christmas like she said she would, but of course, that probably led to her death. Maybe she was safer in Oregon." She sighed.

"Just because there's trouble in a family doesn't mean they don't love one another," I pointed out. "I'm sure Lainey loved you all and was just as frustrated by the trouble between you as you both are. Kids can be complicated."

Grace dabbed at her eyes again with the tissue. "You can say that again. We don't have as much trouble with the boys, but even they have had their moments." She chuckled. "Bryce swore when he was in his teens that he was going to join the army and never return to Maine again. But the older he got, the more he realized the army was never going to satisfy him, and he stayed here on the farm."

I gazed at Frank as he sat there, looking at his hands and intertwining his fingers. He seemed uncomfortable with the conversation. He was probably what some might call stoic. He wasn't one to show emotion, but when your daughter is murdered, those emotions were going to show themselves whether or not you wanted them to.

We sat and talked for a while, and then Lucy and I left, stopping by the farm stand to pick up blueberries before we headed home.

"These blueberries are just beautiful," she said as we carried baskets of berries back to the car. "You're going to make me a cheesecake, aren't you?"

I chuckled. "Of course I'm going to make you a cheesecake. I can hardly wait. I've been dreaming about this cheesecake for days."

I was going to make cheesecakes all right, but we also needed to talk to Jim Martin again.

CHAPTER 8

I was true to my word and spent the rest of the afternoon baking cheesecakes. They were all going to be topped with a sweetened blueberry sauce that I could already taste in my mind. There was something about freshly picked wild blueberries from Maine that were so special nothing could top them. Dixie rubbed up against my legs as I looked over the cooling cheesecakes. "Forget it, Buster, you're not getting any cheesecake."

Dixie meowed, trying to convince me he was starving for some cheesecake, but I would not fall for his ploy. He was cute and all, but sugar wasn't good for him, so he was going to be denied.

I heard the front door open, and I grinned when

Alec entered the kitchen. "Hey there, handsome, how are you doing today?"

He came over to me, wrapped his arms around me, and kissed me. "I'm doing great. How about you?"

I shrugged. "I'm doing all right. I've been busy with cheesecakes."

He nodded. "It's a beautiful sight. I can hardly wait."

"I've got a roast in the oven, and we'll be ready to eat in just a few minutes. I'm glad you could get home early."

"Me too. I'm waiting on lab results on some of the dirt we brought back from where Lainey Easley was found, so I decided I would just wait here at home."

He went to the cupboard and got glasses out, then filled them with ice and got the sweet tea from the refrigerator.

"Any new leads on the case?" I asked as I glanced at the cheesecakes again. I wanted them to cool a little more before I put the blueberry topping on them.

"Not really. I've been talking to everyone, including the farmworkers, but nobody seems to know much of anything as far as who would kill her." The ice in the glasses cracked as he poured sweet tea over them.

I turned toward him. "There were a handful of farmworkers standing in a group talking the morning we found her body. They've got to know something. Didn't they go into that part of the farm? Even if the blueberry bushes were dormant that year, what about this year?"

He nodded and handed me a glass. "It was after the blueberry season when she was murdered. They said they didn't see anything when they worked in the field earlier this year. That would have been before we had all that rain, so it's possible she was still buried, and they just didn't see her body."

I nodded and sighed, then went to the oven and looked at the roast. It smelled heavenly. "I suppose. It just seems like somebody would know something there at the farm."

"I can't argue with you there. I'm still searching. Maybe the dirt we're taking a closer look at will yield some clues."

I grabbed potholders and removed the roast from the oven, setting it on top. The thermometer that was stuck in it showed that it was done, so I gave it a few minutes to rest before cutting into it. I tossed the oven mitts onto the counter and turned to him. "Her father thinks her boyfriend did it, but her mother swears that he was a nice guy, and they only had a casual relationship. Jim Martin. Have you spoken to him?"

He nodded. "He said they broke up in September, and at the time of her death, he was already dating someone else."

I nodded. "Yes, I was surprised to find out he was married. Did he give you any sign of how serious his relationship with Lainey had been?"

He took a sip of his iced tea. "He said he thought he was in love with her, but after they broke up, he realized he wasn't, and soon after he met his future wife."

I sighed. "Darn it. It would be convenient if it was him." I wasn't going to completely rule out that Jim Martin might have killed her. It was early in the investigation, and he might have some surprises for us yet. "Did he tell you about Lainey and her brothers being made to do hard labor when they misbehaved?"

He nodded. "I asked Frank and Grace about it, and they denied it. Maybe she was lying about it."

"Or maybe Jim is because he wants to make you look closer at Frank." Interesting.

"That's possible. I got the lab report back that said her cause of death was blunt force trauma."

I looked at him, one eyebrow raised. "Poor thing. Any idea what was used to kill her?"

"There was a small crowbar found on another part of the farm that we believe is the murder weapon. Unfortunately, it was left out in the elements and there may not be any evidence left behind on it."

I got the butter and milk from the refrigerator to make the mashed potatoes. "What makes you think this is the murder weapon if everything's been washed away?"

"It fits the indentation in her skull."

I shuddered. "I hate she went like that. I hope that Lainey Easley wasn't aware of what was about to happen to her moments before she was murdered." I turned back to him. "Was she hit in the front of her head or the back?"

"The back. Why?"

I nodded and turned back to the potatoes in the pot on the stove. "Good. I'm glad it was the back of her head."

"What do you mean?" he asked incredulously. "The blow killed her. Why does it matter?"

I glanced over my shoulder. "Because maybe she didn't know she was about to die. I think the worst part of being murdered is knowing that it's about to happen."

"Well, you've got a point. If I were going to be murdered, I wouldn't want to know about it in advance."

I shook my head and tossed some butter into the potatoes, mashing them. Next came the milk, salt, and pepper. I wasn't above instant mashed potatoes, but there was nothing like the real thing. It took some extra work, but as far as I was concerned, it was worth it.

"I'm starving."

"Everything will be ready in a matter of minutes," I said, opening the oven to pull out the corn casserole I had made. This was more of a fall meal, but I didn't care. I enjoyed summer, but I loved fall even more, and I was in the mood for a change of seasons. "If you can set this casserole on the table, I'll carve the roast, and we'll be ready to eat."

He grabbed a pair of oven mitts and carried it over for me. I transferred the potatoes to a serving bowl and then carved the roast. The smell of it made me almost lightheaded. I ate a light lunch of salad and had had nothing else to eat since then.

We got the food on the table and sat down to eat

while Dixie sat at my feet, begging for some roast beef.

"If you had to guess, who would you say killed Lainey Easley?"

He thought about this, fork poised above his roast. "She had a lot of trouble with her father."

I gasped. "You don't think he could have killed her?" The thought of Frank killing his daughter made me ill.

He shrugged. "I don't know yet. He's very angry toward her. I think he had his heart set on all of his kids working on the family farm. He said it was what he and his brothers did, and he had always assumed his kids would do the same."

I nodded. "Clem Easley owned the farm when I first moved here with Thaddeus. He was such a sweet man. He loved to talk to all the customers who would come in and buy blueberries from him. I loved going out to the farm, knowing I would get to visit with him for a few minutes. I was so sad when he died. It was about ten years ago, I think."

"Frank doesn't seem to be quite the people person that his father was," Alec said, cutting into the roast on his plate. "This looks good."

"Thank you, and no, Frank isn't very much like his

father. I heard his brothers moved away a few years ago, which surprised me. It's a family farm, after all, and I just assumed they were all happy there. Did he ever mention why they moved?"

He nodded. "Frank said they never enjoyed working on the farm. He said he was disappointed in that, and he was glad they left after their father had died because otherwise it would have killed him."

"Well, if he knew his brothers weren't happy on the farm, why would he expect all three of his children to be happy working there? I haven't spoken to Jason Easley yet. Have you?"

He nodded. "Yes, I've spoken to all of them, and I don't know why Frank thought his kids should be happy working there when his brothers weren't. I think being raised on a farm can make you either love it or hate it. I could see a lot of kids wanting to escape it, so maybe he shouldn't be so surprised that his daughter wanted nothing to do with it."

"Exactly," I said, cutting into my roast. I had gotten it to just the perfect doneness, still a bit pink, but not as rare as some people make it because I wanted to know it was done.

I made a mental note to speak with both of Lainey's brothers and see what they had to say.

CHAPTER 9

ucy and I stopped by the blueberry farm again, hoping we might run into Bryce or Jason Easley. We had questions for them that I was hoping they would be willing to answer.

"That cheesecake you brought by the house yesterday was delicious, by the way," Lucy said.

I chuckled as I found a parking spot and we got out of the car. "You've told me that at least six times today."

Grinning, she replied, "I just want you to know how good it was. I appreciate it when you make something for Ed and me."

I nodded and slung my purse over my shoulder. We had brought along baskets just in case we had a reason to pick blueberries. "Well, you are more than welcome. I appreciate you telling me how much you enjoy my baked goods, especially the cheesecake because I think I outdid myself with it."

"Oh, you certainly did. If we get more blueberries, you'll make another cheesecake, right?"

I laughed. "Wait, you don't mean to tell me you and Ed ate that entire cheesecake?"

She shook her head without looking at me. "No, but you can bet it won't be around for much longer."

I grinned as we walked along the paved path that led out to the blueberry fields. "Do you see either of them?" I glanced around as we walked, trying not to look suspicious. I wanted it to seem as if we just happened to run into them if we saw them.

"No, I don't see them. Is the blueberry field where we found Lainey still taped off?"

"I don't think so. Alec tries to gather his evidence quickly so that people outside the investigation don't get a chance to disturb it." Even though an officer would have been staked out at the field overnight, Alec wouldn't leave a crime scene for long until all the evidence was collected.

As we walked along, a white pickup drove toward us on the path. When it got closer, I shielded my eyes against the sun so I could see the driver better. It was just our luck that Bryce Easley was driving it. I waved at him, and he slowed the truck and pulled over. Lucy and I hurried up to the window as he rolled it down.

"Good morning, Bryce," I said. "I'm so sorry about Lainey."

"Yes, I'm sorry too," Lucy said.

He gave a curt nod of his head. "Thank you. I appreciate hearing that. I still can't get over the fact that she was found right out in that blueberry field. Actually, I can't get over the fact that she's really and truly gone." He sighed.

"Losing a loved one is so hard," I said. "It takes a long time to stop expecting to hear from them or see them walk through the door." When my first husband was killed by a drunk driver, my kids and I had been devastated beyond words. But it was the expectation that I would hear from him again, only to immediately remember he was gone, and I would never hear his voice again, that was the hardest to get through.

He nodded, his eyes focusing on the steering wheel in front of him. "Yeah, even though Lainey was kind of a flake, I still expected to hear from her from time to time. I figured she would grow up and rejoin the family again one day."

"Things were that bad?" Lucy asked.

He looked at her and nodded. "Yeah, they were pretty bad. Lainey and my dad used to fight a lot when she was in high school, and she swore she would leave this Podunk town and never set foot on this blueberry farm again. She kind of did that when she moved out and got her own place a couple of years after high school. We didn't see a lot of her in those years. Then, when she up and moved to Oregon, I was worried I really might not see her again. And I didn't."

"If you don't mind me asking, why did Lainey have such a hard time getting along with your family?" I hoped he didn't think I was being too forward, but I needed to know.

He frowned. "My dad can be hard to get along with. I think that's what started it, but then, Lainey has always had a chip on her shoulder. She always blew things out of proportion and thought people were picking on her." He rolled his eyes, but he was smiling when he did it. "She was a good kid, but she just kind of lost her way, I guess."

"Bryce, did your father punish you kids by making you work on the farm?" I asked. I wondered what his take was on what Jim had said.

He gave me a lopsided grin. "Sure, if we got out of line, he would make us hoe weeds or something. But he didn't break any child labor laws. Why?"

I shrugged. "I just wondered. Do you have any idea what might have happened to Lainey?"

He looked toward the nearby blueberry field before answering. Then he turned back to us. "I don't know. I've been going over things in my mind since her body was found, and I can't put my finger on anything. Except maybe for one person she had trouble with."

When he didn't continue, I said, "One person?"

"Yeah, and I hate even saying it out loud because it's an awful thing to say about somebody, especially when it's about somebody who has been a loyal employee for so many years."

This piqued my interest. "When Alec was here investigating, there were a handful of farm workers standing off to the side talking."

He nodded. "Yeah, I saw them, but the person I'm talking about wasn't among them." He shook his head. "I really shouldn't say anything."

"I imagine it would be hard if you thought he was loyal to your family, and then you thought maybe you had made a mistake about that," Lucy said.

He glanced at her and licked his bottom lip. "It's Eli Thompson."

"Eli Thompson? He's worked here for a lot of years, hasn't he?" I asked.

He nodded. "Forty years. He used to work for my grandfather when he owned the farm. Eli has been like a member of the family for years. Well, a distant member of the family, I guess. It always seems like it's painful to him when we try to include him at holiday get-togethers." He chuckled. "He's like that uncle who's never quite sure what to do when other people are around. That's what makes me feel so bad about having these thoughts."

"Why would you suspect him?" I asked.

He gazed at me for a moment before answering. "When Lainey didn't show up for Christmas the year before last, he asked my mom about her. She told him she hadn't heard from her, even though she promised to come. My mom was still upset about it, and I guess he could tell she was. She said he behaved strangely. He shifted his weight from side to side, and he had a hat in his hand that he was wringing as he spoke to her. He suddenly seemed incredibly nervous, and she asked him if he was feeling okay. He told her he was sorry, then abruptly left. We kind of forgot about it, but in the last few months, he's been disappearing in the middle of his shift. I've caught him in that field, where Lainey's body was found several times."

This seemed odd. "Caught him doing what?"

He shook his head. "Sometimes he's on his phone. Or sometimes he's just standing out there doing nothing. I've asked him what was going on, but he gets flustered and won't give me a straight answer. At first, I just thought he was Eli being Eli. But now that Lainey's body has been found, I have to wonder if there was a sinister reason he was out there."

"That does sound strange," Lucy agreed.

"Did you talk to my husband about that?" I asked.

He nodded. "I just went to his office to talk to him this morning. I couldn't bring myself to do it any earlier. It would be absolutely crushing to my family if he was Lainey's killer."

"But what would his reason be for killing her?" I asked.

He shook his head and shrugged. "I wish I had an answer to that question. I honestly don't know why he would do it. And that's why it gives me a little hope that I'm wrong about it. I can hope, anyway, because I feel a little like I've betrayed a member of the family." He frowned.

"I can see why you would feel that way," I said. "That's a long time for a person to be working anywhere these days, and combined with the fact that this is a family-run business, of course he's going to feel like family." My heart went out to Bryce. I don't know what I would have done if I were in his shoes, but if I felt strongly that Eli might have had something to do with the murder of my sister, it would be hard to continue working with him.

"Lainey really didn't like the farm?" I asked.

He chuckled softly. "No, Lainey really didn't like the farm. She liked dressing up, wearing nail polish, and high heels. Dressing that way isn't conducive to farming." He chuckled again. "But then, my brother Jason doesn't enjoy the farm much, either. I don't know why. But I had my own moments when I was in high school when I thought for sure I would leave this place behind, but the older I got, the more I realized how much I loved it. Farming is in my blood."

"Small businesses are special, and family farms are even more so," Lucy said.

He smiled and nodded. "Well ladies, I hate to run, but I'm going up to the house to check on my mom and see how she's doing today. This has been hard on her."

"I can't even imagine how difficult this has to be for all of you," I said. "It was nice getting to talk to you, Bryce. I'm sorry again about Lainey."

He nodded again. "I appreciate hearing that."

"Give your mother our best," Lucy said.

We stepped out of the way as he drove off down the road.

"That's so sad," Lucy said with a sigh.

I nodded. "I agree."

It was sad that Lainey had been murdered, but even sadder if an employee who the family regarded as one of their own ended up being the killer.

CHAPTER 10

*L*ucy and I picked up more blueberries while we were at the farm, and after dropping Lucy off at home, I headed to the grocery store to pick up more cream cheese. I hadn't brought the officers at the police station anything in more than a month, and I was thinking about making some mini cheesecakes to take to them.

I was pushing my buggy into the dairy section when I saw Jason Easley pushing a buggy toward me. Jason was Frank and Grace's middle child. He looked sad and forlorn as he pushed his shopping cart aimlessly, and I felt sorry for him. I picked up four packages of cream cheese and put them into my cart.

"Hello, Jason," I said when I got closer to him. "I'm so sorry about Lainey."

He stopped pushing his buggy and sighed. "Thank you, Allie. I sure appreciate hearing that."

He was dressed in well-worn jeans and a white T-shirt, but his feet were clad in flip-flops, making me wonder if he had the day off from the farm. "I spoke to your mom and dad the other day. I know this has to be so hard for all of you."

He nodded as his eyes welled up, but he blinked back the tears. "I never in a million years would have thought something like this would happen to Lainey. Or anyone else in my family, for that matter. I thought for sure she would give us a call one day and tell us what she had been up to since we last spoke to her. But that's never going to happen now."

I wanted to hug him. He looked so miserable, but as we stood there, other shoppers pushed their buggies in and out of the dairy department, and I would have had to step in front of them to do that. "Jason, do you have any idea who might have wanted to harm your sister?"

He shook his head. "No. Lainey was one of those girls who was a little high-strung, but she was always sweet to everyone. She went out of her way to check on people or to see if they needed anything."

This didn't sound like the same girl who was causing her family so much anguish before she disappeared. "I knew Lainey, but not well. She seemed like a sweet girl."

He nodded. "Yeah, she was. I was six years old when my mom brought her home from the hospital, and I thought she was a gift for me." He chuckled. "She was the pinkest baby I'd ever seen, and I couldn't wait until she could play with me and my trucks."

My heart melted. "Oh, my goodness, that's so sweet. Bryce is older than you, isn't he? Did he feel the same way about the new baby?"

He snorted and shook his head. "No, not Bryce. To be honest, Bryce was mad that my parents brought a baby home. He complained about her crying all the time, which she did, but it's not like she could help it."

"Sometimes older siblings can be jealous of a new baby. I bet they got along later though, when she was older."

He shook his head. "No, those two always fought like cats and dogs. It was Bryce's fault because he teased her all the time. And if she would snap back at him, it made him angry."

"Oh, that's a shame," I said. "I always got along with my younger siblings. Like you, I thought they were gifts my parents brought home for me, and they were a lot of fun to play with."

He leaned on his buggy. "Well, you have to realize that Bryce was my parents' favorite. He was older, and he helped a lot on the farm by the time Lainey came around. And then my mother paid so much attention to her because she needed the attention, and that made him angry. But he's just as broken up over her death as the rest of us. It just seems like it can't be real."

"Had you spoken to your sister before she disappeared?" I asked and picked up two more packages of cream cheese and set them in my cart.

"I talked to her before she left to go to Oregon. I asked her to come home for Christmas, and she said she would try. Then my parents paid for a ticket, and she said she was definitely coming. When she didn't show up, I was heartbroken. I texted her and called her over and over in the weeks after her disappearance."

"The calls just went to voicemail?"

He shook his head. "Not at first. At first, it just rang and rang before going to voicemail. I figured maybe she got mad or got her feelings hurt about something and she was just being difficult. But after a few weeks, the calls started going immediately to voicemail, and I never got to speak to her again." The tears in his eyes were back, but he blinked them away just as quickly as he had the first time.

"I'm so sorry. That just breaks my heart for you."

He nodded his appreciation. "Thanks. I wish I could have one more chance to talk to her and tell her I love her."

"I'm sure she knew, Jason. Did any of your family get to talk to her after Christmas?" I asked gently and picked up two more packages of cream cheese.

He shook his head. "No, none of us had any contact with her."

I sighed. "I'm so sorry."

"When she didn't come home for Christmas, I also searched social media for her. I found several accounts that were hers, and I messaged her there too, but of course, she never answered me. I still go back and check them from time to time, but she completely stopped posting anything after December twentieth."

"The twentieth? And her plane arrived on the twenty-first?"

He nodded, glancing into my shopping cart which now held a total of ten packages of cream cheese. I was debating how much more I should pick up. "Yeah, her plane was supposed to come in on the twenty-first. I figured she got here, and something happened to her. It had to have been a stranger because no one who knew her would have done something so terrible to her."

"Where was she supposed to be staying when she got here?" I asked.

"She was supposed to be staying with my parents. They offered to pick her up at the airport, but she said a friend would pick her up. When she didn't show up that night, we just assumed they probably went out to do something in the evening and it got late. I called around, but no one had seen her."

"That's odd," I said. "You would think she would have been in contact with her friends since she was going to have a few days here before returning home."

"Yeah, we were surprised by that at first. And then, I'll be honest and admit that we were hurt and a little angry when she never showed up at Christmas time. We thought she had just run off with one of her friends who I hadn't spoken to and couldn't be bothered with us. I'm so ashamed for even thinking that."

"You shouldn't be ashamed of that. You knew she had her issues, and it would have been understandable to think she had taken off with a friend instead of coming to spend Christmas with the family." Speaking to Jason just broke my heart. He seemed to love his sister and was devastated about what had happened to her.

He nodded but glanced away. He looked as if he were on the verge of breaking down right there in the grocery store.

Taking a deep breath, he turned back to me and looked at the cream cheese in my cart. "I guess you're going to be doing some baking?"

"Oh yes, I'm making cheesecakes, and I'm using the blueberries from your family's farm to make the topping."

He smiled now. "Well, I sure love a good cheesecake, especially when our blueberries are in the topping. I'm going to have to learn how to bake one. My mom makes them sometimes, but not nearly often enough."

"Oh, my goodness, then I'll have to make you a cheesecake. I'm making several of them anyway, so I'll get some more cream cheese." I picked up two more packages and then grabbed another two.

He laughed. "Oh Allie, you don't have to do that. I'm sure cheesecakes are a lot of work."

I shook my head. "I'm already making some, so making an extra one won't be a problem. Do you still live there on the farm?"

He nodded. "Yes, there are a couple of smaller houses behind the main house, and I live in the smallest one. I've taken a few days off work, trying to get myself together since finding out Lainey is dead, and Bryce just hates it. He doesn't understand why I would need to take any time off from the farm. But sometimes you just need a break."

"I don't blame you one bit. You're grieving for your sister, and you need time off. Some people deal with their grief by throwing themselves into their work, and that's probably what he's doing, but you shouldn't feel bad about taking time off and just trying to rest."

He nodded. "Yeah, he's not going to make me feel guilty about it. I'm going to take the time off, and that's that. Well, Allie, you don't have to make me a cheesecake, but I'd sure appreciate it if you do. I've got to pick up a few more things and then head back to the house. My mom wants me to go with her to the funeral home to make arrangements." He grimaced. "I'm dreading that."

"Oh gosh," I said. "I'm so sorry the two of you have to do that. Can I hug you?" I couldn't help it. He needed one.

He nodded sheepishly, and I scooted my cart over and stepped in the way of an older woman, but I didn't care. I hugged Jason in hopes it might make him feel the tiniest bit better.

CHAPTER 11

he following morning, Lucy and I stopped by the Cup and Bean Coffee Shop after our run. I had relayed everything I had learned about Lainey and her family to Alec the previous night. I would have liked to say he was close to finding the killer. He wasn't. But I had the utmost confidence there would be a break in the case soon.

"I'm going to get an iced caramel latte," Lucy said, looking up at the menu board. "Fall will be here before you know it, and it will be too cold to drink iced coffees."

I nodded. "Then we'd better enjoy our iced coffee while we can. But I'm more than ready for a pumpkin spice latte."

She groaned. "Oh, don't say that. It's all I've been thinking about for weeks now, and you know we can't have one for several more weeks."

I nodded, and we stepped up to the counter and gave the barista our orders. Then I turned to Lucy. "I've been experimenting with making my own pumpkin spice lattes. They're okay, but they're not the same as getting them at a coffee shop."

"At least you're daring enough to try," she said. "All I do is sit around and dream about them. Well, honestly, I'm dreaming about pumpkin spice anything." She chuckled.

"Me too. When I get done with these blueberry cheesecakes I'm making, maybe I'll make some pumpkin cream cheese muffins."

She groaned. "Now you're torturing me. You've got to make them. I need one."

I paid for our iced coffees, and we headed over to Mr. Winters' table. "Good morning, Mr. Winters."

He looked up from his newspaper and pushed his glasses back up on his nose. "Good morning, ladies. What's new?"

We sat down across from him, and Lucy reached underneath the table and patted Sadie's head. "Unfortunately, not enough. Have you found out anything?" I asked.

He pressed his lips together. "I wish I had something big. I still feel terrible that the Easley's daughter was murdered. But I was thinking; if she arrived in town for Christmas, how come no one saw her?"

I shook my head. "That is an excellent question, but unfortunately, it's one we don't have an answer to yet. But we'll figure it out."

Lucy took a sip of her coffee. "Yes, we'll figure it out. I think it's strange that nobody will admit to having seen her, so my guess is the killer saw her and doesn't want to let anyone know they did. They're trying to distance themselves from her completely."

"I think you're right," I said. "We know she arrived in town for Christmas, so maybe the friend who picked her up from the airport is her killer."

"So, who picked her up from the airport?" Mr. Winters asked.

I shook my head. "She only told her parents a friend was picking her up. She never mentioned a name."

I glanced up when I saw someone heading in our direction. It was Dave Evans, the Easley Farms manager. I smiled at him. "Hey, Dave, how are you?"

He nodded, one hand in the pocket of his windbreaker, the other holding a cup of coffee. He was dressed in fancy blue jeans with a crease down the middle. I hadn't seen anybody press their jeans in years, and I was pretty sure those jeans had never seen a day of hard work on the farm.

He smiled. "Hello, everyone. I'm doing well, and I hope you all are too. Allie, I spoke with your husband the other day when you ladies found Lainey's body among the blueberries. It was a sad day for all of us."

I nodded. "It's sad that someone killed Lainey."

"I'm glad your husband is on the case; I've heard nothing but good things about him. Does he have any leads yet? Is he going to make an arrest soon?" he asked almost eagerly.

I was a little surprised he was asking this question. Most people beat around the bush for a while before asking if Alec had someone in mind as the killer. "If he has his eye on someone, he hasn't mentioned it to me. He doesn't tell me everything he knows about a case."

A look of disappointment flashed across his face, and then he said, "No, I suppose he can't. But I know Frank and Grace are simply brokenhearted about this whole thing, as you can imagine. I was just hoping that your husband was getting ready to arrest someone, so at least they would have some sense of justice."

Lucy nodded. "I think not knowing who the killer is makes it so much harder."

"It would drive me crazy," Mr. Winters added.

Dave nodded. "Yes, exactly. Grace doesn't look like she's gotten a wink of sleep since the body was found. And Frank just walks around muttering to himself. I know having the killer arrested isn't going to solve all their problems, but I think it would help."

"Dave, how long have you worked for the Easleys?" I asked, taking a sip of my coffee.

"Oh, right at about eighteen years now. It's the best job I've ever had, and I really want the Easleys to have closure. They're like family." He took a sip of his coffee.

"I bet when you work for someone for that long they do become family," I said. "Have you been there the longest?" I already knew the answer, but I didn't want to draw too much attention to what I knew. I couldn't have him thinking I was overly interested in the farm employees.

He shook his head, grinning. "Oh no, that honor belongs to Eli Thompson. He's been there for forty years. I swear, I don't think he's ever going to retire. Not that he's all that old. I think he's only around sixty-two or so."

"Must be a good job to have worked there that long," Mr. Winters said.

"The Easleys treat their employees well. It's nice to work at a place where you're respected and thought well of. It's the best job I've ever had," he said.

"Did you see much of Lainey when she lived at home?" I asked, taking another sip of my coffee. He had to have known her well, didn't he?

He nodded. "Oh, of course. Lainey worked in the office for a little while, if you could call it that." He smirked. "They thought if they gave her a job, it would help straighten out her attitude, but it didn't do a thing for her. I think it actually made it worse."

"What do you mean?" Lucy asked, setting her cup down.

His brow furrowed. "Look, I know the Easleys loved their daughter, but some of us at the farm didn't care much for her. She had an attitude. Once, when she was hired to do a little filing and typing around the office, she let it go to her head and started giving orders to the farm workers. Can you imagine it? She had no business doing something like that, but she did it anyway. We tried to ignore her, but she could get mean when we did that."

Why would Lainey think she could give orders to the other employees? "What did Frank say about that?" I asked.

He shook his head and made a face. "Frank did his best to pretend it wasn't happening. He only gave her the job because her mother insisted. It would have been nice if it had helped straighten out her problems, but like I said, it didn't. Just between the four of us, I didn't trust her. She was moody, too."

"What did she do to make you not trust her?" I couldn't imagine how having a job where you filed or typed would put you in a position to lose someone's trust.

He stepped a little closer and leaned forward. "One day I returned a little early from lunch and caught her rummaging through Frank's desk."

Lucy gasped. "No!"

He nodded. "Yes. Caught with her hand in the cookie jar. The drawer she was rummaging through had the checkbook in it. And she knew that's where it was kept."

"Well, I'll be," Mr. Winters said. "You think she was trying to steal from her own father?"

He shrugged. "When I walked through the door I startled her, and she jumped and nearly screamed. She said she was looking for some white-out because she had made a mistake while typing up an envelope. I'm afraid Frank Easley hasn't come into the 21st century with computers and was having her type up all his envelopes for sending out payments to vendors and such." He smirked.

"Do you think there's a chance she was telling the truth?" I asked. "All she was doing was looking for white-out?"

He shook his head. "No. She normally sat at the secretary's desk. There was a bottle of white-out sitting right there on top of it. When I pointed that out, she got embarrassed and made an excuse, saying she hadn't even noticed it. Honestly, that girl was trouble. Not only was she willing to steal from her father by forging checks, but she also acted like she owned the place. If she had hung around that farm much longer, she would have run it into the ground."

"*Did* she forge any checks?" I asked.

He shook his head. "Not that I know of. But if she had, I don't know if Frank would have told me. His wife favored the girl, and Frank would do anything for his wife. So I'm sure he would have covered it up if it had happened."

"Who do you think killed her?" I asked.

He shrugged. "I have my thoughts, but for now I'm keeping them to myself."

I almost sighed in exasperation, but this was interesting, and I wondered now why Frank seemed so angry with Lainey. *Had* she forged some checks? Was there a reason she moved to Oregon other than just wanting to leave Sandy Harbor? Maybe Frank had caught her stealing and had told her she had to leave or else. And then she had returned to the scene of the crime. Interesting indeed.

CHAPTER 12

W hen I parked at Easley's Blueberry Farm, Lucy turned and looked at me, squinting, but not saying anything.

I turned to her. "What's that look for?"

She shrugged. "You've been quiet the whole drive over. What's going through that mind of yours?"

I laughed. "You know me. I'm like a bloodhound when we're gathering information about a murder. It's all I can think about."

She nodded. "I know you are. I feel the same way. What do you think about what Dave told us yesterday?"

"I think I'd love to get Eli alone so I can talk to him. And I'm wondering if he's still returning to that

KATHLEEN SUZETTE

field where Lainey's body was found. Maybe we can talk to him today."

You could say that Lucy and I might be addicted to hunting down clues to the various murders that had occurred over the years. But you couldn't fault us for that. Once we had our first taste of crime solving back when I first met Alec, we were hooked.

She nodded as we got out of the car. "I think that's a great plan. Let's just mosey on past the fruit stand and back to that field. If anyone asks what we're doing back there, we'll just do what we did the first time we came out here. Say we didn't know we weren't supposed to go that far back."

We got on the little paved path and walked past the blueberry stand. There were a handful of customers waiting in line to buy fresh-picked blue-berries and other produce. In the other sections of fields, we could see a person here or there picking blueberries as we walked, but there weren't many people out today. That was a good thing. I hoped to find Eli by himself.

An enormous cloud scudded past the sun, blocking out its rays for a minute, but as soon as it moved, the sky brightened again. I glanced skyward. "I heard we're supposed to get some rain tomorrow."

"We could use some. Other than that big heavy rain last month, the summer has been kind of dry."

The past spring had been wetter than normal, and after the big storm last month, I would have sworn we were going to have a very wet summer, but it hadn't happened. I enjoyed a rainy summer day, and I missed it.

The further we walked, the fewer people we saw. I was hopeful we would run into Eli. I looked at the bushes as we passed and noticed the further we went, the more blueberries there were, as these bushes hadn't been harvested yet. Lucy elbowed me, and I glanced at her.

As hoped, Eli was walking down the path toward us. He was wearing Wellington boots, a red and black plaid shirt, and faded jeans.

I smiled at him. "Good morning, Eli!" I called while he was still some distance from us.

He looked puzzled for a moment, then nodded. "Oh, hello. You ladies have gone too far. If you've come to pick blueberries, you need to go back the other way."

Lucy and I stopped, and I glanced at the bushes to my right. "Oh? Why is that? I thought all the blueberries were ready to be picked."

He shook his head. "The ones closer to the farm stand ripen earliest. Most of these aren't quite ready yet."

I turned to Lucy, trying to look surprised. "Well, my goodness, I guess we walked further than we thought we did."

Lucy nodded. "It's such a beautiful day. I guess we got carried away walking down the path."

Eli stopped in front of us. "Yeah, I think you're going to find better blueberries down there. Some of these are still green and won't be ripe for another couple of weeks. It's best if you let us harvest these blueberries because we pick the ripe ones first and sell them at the shack."

"That's good to know," I said. "Eli, how have you been? I haven't seen you in forever."

He shrugged. "Oh, I guess I'm doing about as well as can be expected." He glanced up at the sky. "Might get some rain."

"Eli, haven't you worked here for a very long time? You were here when I married my first husband years ago," I said.

He smiled. "Oh yeah, I've been working here about forty years now, so I was here back then. I remember Thaddeus. He was a good guy."

"He was one of the best. He always said you would make sure we got the very best wild blueberries when we came here, and he was right." I liked Eli, and I hoped he didn't have anything to do with Lainey's death.

He shoved his hands into the pockets of his jeans. "I certainly do my best."

"You must really enjoy your job here," Lucy said. "That's a long time to work anywhere."

He grimaced, glancing off past my shoulder. "Well, I really enjoyed working for Clem and his wife. Those were Frank's parents, you know. They were good people."

"Yes, I knew his parents had started the farm years ago. How do you like working for Frank and Grace?" The look on his face said he didn't enjoy working for them as much as he did for Clem.

He shrugged. "Oh, it's okay."

There was something he wasn't saying. Eli was a man of few words most of the time, and you had to read between the lines with him, and there was something between those lines.

"You're not looking to retire anytime soon?" Lucy asked. "We'd miss you here on the farm."

He smiled again. "Well, to be honest, I've been

thinking about it. I haven't decided when I'm going to do it, but I'm sixty-two now, and I figure I'm due for a nice long vacation."

"Sixty-two? You don't look a day over fifty," I said.

He laughed. "Oh, now you're just trying to flatter me. You don't have to do that to get me to pick the best blueberries for you. I'll do it, anyway."

I shook my head. "I mean it. You look young for your age, and you always know which blueberries are going to be the best. Eli, we were here when Lainey's body was found last week."

He frowned. "I am absolutely gutted about it. I can't imagine who would do something like that to her. She was a sweet girl. I watched her grow up, and it just makes me sick that somebody killed her."

The look on Eli's face told me he was sincere. At least, I hoped he was. "I think it's been a shock for everyone who knew her. I've never heard a bad thing said about her." That may have been a lie since Dave had already told us he thought she was stealing from her father, but I had trouble believing that, too.

He nodded. "Yeah, it's just awful. Is your husband working on the case?"

"Yes, Alec is on the case. I wish he had more to go on, but it seems there isn't much just yet."

"I might retire sooner rather than later," Eli suddenly said, bringing the conversation back around.

"Oh? Why is that?" I asked, hoping he would enlighten us with anything that might help with the case.

He inhaled before answering. "Just between the three of us, I overheard Dave Evans telling Frank that Lainey was trouble for the farm. He said she would destroy it if he ever turned it over to her."

"Was Frank going to turn the farm over to her?" Lucy asked.

"He and Grace talked some about retiring early and turning the farm over to the kids. I think Bryce would do a good job running the place, but I couldn't see Lainey or Jason taking all that much interest in it. But I hated to hear him talk about her that way. She was a good kid. Young and immature, but good. Dave couldn't stand her, so I guess I shouldn't have been surprised."

"What did Frank say when he told him that about her?" I asked.

Eli shrugged. "I had to get back to work, so I left before I heard his answer. But like I said, Lainey was a good girl. From the time she was real little until the last I saw her, I always liked her. And I think it takes a lot of nerve to go to her father and tell him she would destroy the family farm that he and his father worked so hard to build. Dave doesn't know how things would go if she and her brothers took over. I'm sure it would work out."

"It takes a lot of nerve to say something like that to her father," I said.

"If I had a kid, and somebody came to me complaining about them, I would put them in their place," Lucy agreed.

I nodded. "I hope that's what he did."

Eli frowned. "I think Dave was worried about his job, and that's why he said it. Dave is real cunning that way. Seems like he's always got an angle. Manipulative."

"Hasn't Dave worked here a long time, too?" I asked. I wondered how Eli felt working with someone he didn't think much of for as long as he had.

He nodded. "Yeah, I think he's been here around seventeen or eighteen years. I forget. But he started out as a regular farmhand and somehow got promoted to farm manager. Never particularly cared for him, so I suppose I shouldn't even talk about him because I won't say anything nice. But that's why I'm thinking retiring sooner is probably better than later. I don't need drama in my life at my age."

"I hear you," I said. "The older I get, the less drama I want in my life."

He gave me a quick nod and looked down the path past us. "Well, I guess I better get going. Those blueberries won't pick themselves."

"No, they sure won't," I said. But he made no move to leave.

He turned back to us. "Lainey and Bryce didn't get along much of the time, either. I never could put my finger on what the trouble was." He shrugged. "I guess siblings have trouble sometimes."

"That's the truth," Lucy said.

He smiled. "Well, I better get going. See you ladies around."

"We'll just head back to the bushes near the farm stand and get our blueberries there," I told him.

"It was nice talking to you, ladies. Have a good day."

We turned and walked slowly behind him as he strode down the paved path.

"That's odd that Dave complained about Lainey to

her father," Lucy whispered when the distance between us and Eli had lengthened.

"It sure is, and it has me wondering about Dave."

It also had me wondering about Frank. Why would he put up with Dave speaking that way about his daughter? Or had he shut him down as he should? And Bryce? Had his jealousy of his little sister gotten the best of him?

aking cheesecake is an art. The ingredients must be measured precisely, or you might end up with a grainy texture. If the water bath is skipped, or the temperature and baking time isn't right, you end up with cavernous cracks in the middle. I didn't make cheesecake often, but when I did, I did it up big. There's nothing like the cool, creamy taste and texture of a good cheesecake. Sour cream was just one of my secret weapons for a delicious cheesecake. The freshly picked wild blueberries from the Easley's farm made into a delicious blueberry topping was another.

I went all out with my cheesecake baking and made four dozen mini cheesecakes in muffin tins to take down to the officers at the police department. They appreciated anything I baked, so it was a pleasure making these for them.

"Is Alec expecting us?" Lucy asked as we carried the bakery boxes of mini cheesecakes into the building. We each held two boxes of the creamy delights.

I shook my head as I balanced my boxes and reached over to pull the heavy glass door open. "No, I wasn't sure if I was going to get them all finished this morning. We'll call this a pleasant surprise for him."

Ted Garrett, a police force veteran, was manning the front counter. He looked up at us, and when he spied the bakery boxes, he grinned. "Well, good morning, Allie. Good morning, Lucy. What's that you're carrying?"

I smiled back at him. "Mini cheesecakes." I set my boxes on the counter. "You like cheesecake, don't you, Ted?"

He brightened. "Are you kidding me? Of course I love cheesecake. What kind is it? No, don't even bother telling me. It doesn't matter what kind it is, because I know it's going to be delicious if you made it."

"Allie always makes the tastiest baked goods," Lucy said.

"Now you two are embarrassing me," I said. "But I think these cheesecakes turned out particularly well. And to answer your question, they're blueberry cheesecakes with a vanilla cookie crust."

His eyebrows shot up. "Vanilla cookie crust? Oh, that sounds so good."

I nodded and opened one of the boxes. "I like graham cracker crust, but to be honest, I prefer a cookie crust, and the vanilla complements the blueberry cheesecake better. You'd better grab a couple of these before we take them to the back, or you may not see them again."

"You don't need to tell me twice." He reached into the box and removed two of the little cheesecakes. I used silver foil baking cups and the blueberry topping paired with the silver perfectly. "Allie, these look delicious. Thank you so much for thinking of us."

"You're welcome, Ted. You all work so hard in this town, and it's a pleasure for me to make something that will brighten your day."

He eyed the two cheesecakes hungrily. "And our day is absolutely brightened by these. Thank you so much."

I closed the top of the box and picked up both boxes again. "Can we go back?"

He hit the button that would unlock the doors leading back to the offices with his elbow, as his hands were busy peeling back the foil liner from a mini cheesecake. "There you go."

"Thanks!" I called over my shoulder as we headed down the narrow hallway which led to the break room. But first, I stopped at Alec's door and knocked with the toe of my shoe.

"Come in!" he called.

After fumbling with the doorknob on our side, he opened the door for me. "Well, what do we have here?"

I grinned. "Cheesecakes. You'd better grab a couple if you want any."

He lifted the lid off the top box and grabbed two of them. "You're such a good wife." He gave me a quick kiss.

"I know," I said with a grin, and Lucy and I headed to the break room to put the boxes out for the other officers.

"Hi, Alec!" Lucy called over her shoulder.

"Hi, Lucy!" he replied before returning to his office.

The break room was empty when we set the boxes on one of the tables, but I knew that as soon as word got around about the treats, it would fill up quickly. We headed back to Alec's office and took a seat in front of his desk.

Alec nodded; his mouth full of cheesecake. When he swallowed, he said, "These are the best cheesecakes ever. You should make them more often."

I chuckled. "I know, I need to do that. What's going on with the case?"

He took a sip of the black coffee in the Styrofoam cup on his desk and made a face. "That coffee is swill. I talked to Eli first thing this morning, but he didn't seem to have much to say."

"What do you mean?" I asked. I had told him last night that Lucy and I spoke to Eli at the farm, and Alec had said he was going to drop by this morning to speak to him.

He nodded. "I asked him about his relationship with the Easleys, and he said it was fine, but he wouldn't go in-depth about anything."

"Really? He was very open with us yesterday," Lucy said.

He nodded. "He clammed up with me. He told me everything was just fine on the farm."

"Did you ask him about Bryce seeing him hanging out in the field where Lainey's body was found?" I asked. I had wanted to ask him myself, but I didn't want to make him suspicious. He would have known someone was talking about him if I had brought it up.

"Yes, I asked him about that, and he claims he was simply checking up on the blueberry bushes. He said they weren't ripening as quickly as they should have been, and he was concerned they wouldn't be ready as planned."

"When we started picking blueberries that day, they looked fine to us," I said. "Of course, I was trying to get Lilly to pick some berries, so it's not like I had time to look at them carefully."

"But they looked really good," Lucy added.

"I pointed that out, and he said it wasn't unusual for some of the berries to ripen faster than the majority, and what you saw and picked were probably the ripe ones." He took another bite of his cheesecake.

I didn't like the sound of this. I liked Eli, and I hoped he had nothing to do with the murder. But if he didn't, why wasn't he more forthcoming with Alec?

"Do you feel like he had something to do with the murder?" I asked him.

He was quiet for a moment as he thought about it. "I can't really say. If it's true he was hanging out there for no good reason, then it certainly makes me suspicious, but that doesn't mean he's the murderer." He sighed and took another bite of his cheesecake.

"What about Dave?" I asked. "If he was as resentful of Lainey as Eli seems to believe, then maybe it was him."

"Eli says Frank relies on Dave to manage everything happening at the farm. When I asked him if he thought Dave might have wanted to hurt Lainey, he was quick to say there was no way Dave could have done anything to her." He shrugged. "He didn't seem to think he would hurt her."

"That's not what he told us," I protested. "He said Dave couldn't stand Lainey."

"I know," he said.

"What about Frank?" Lucy asked. "It seems he had his own issues with his daughter."

He took a bite of his cheesecake before answering. "I'm keeping my eye on him as well."

I sighed. "That poor girl. I just keep thinking about her and how awful it must have been in the moments before she was murdered."

He nodded. "I know what you mean. I just wish we could find her phone. I think there has to be more clues there."

"What about the key you found?" I asked. "Did you ever figure out what it went to?"

He shook his head. "No, I gave the key back to her mother. I told her if she could figure out what it belonged to, it might have some answers for us, but I don't have any idea what it went to yet."

"She didn't have any idea, either?" I asked.

"No, she couldn't think of a thing, but she said she would take it and look into it."

"You have to wonder what it could go to," Lucy said.

Alec took the last bite of his first cheesecake and closed his eyes. After he swallowed, he said, "Delicious. Absolutely delicious. I would love to know what that key is for. She didn't have a car here in town, and the key was too small for that, anyway. It could be for something back in Oregon and probably is. Maybe a storage locker or a padlock on her back gate." He opened his eyes and shrugged. "We may never find out what that key is for."

I hated that we still didn't know who had killed Lainey, and I hoped something would come to light soon. And why had Eli changed his story when talking to Alec? Was he afraid Dave would find out what he had said about him?

CHAPTER 14

There was a knock on Alec's office door, and then it swung open. The police chief, Ben Tiller, poked his head inside. "I don't mean to disturb you all, but Allie, these cheesecakes are delicious. I snagged one to bring home to Anita."

"Oh Ben, you're so sweet. I'm glad you like them, and I'm glad you got one for Anita. You might need to bring her two." I winked.

He chuckled. "You know what? You might be right. I might need to bring a couple home for myself too. For later. But that would be kind of greedy, wouldn't it?"

"There's no such thing as being greedy when we're

talking about Allie's blueberry cheesecake," Lucy informed him.

He laughed again. "You've got a point there, Lucy. Alec, I'm envious that you get all of Allie's baked goods. Anita only bakes around the holidays."

"Holiday baking is the best kind of baking," I said with a chuckle. "I guess I need to bring in baked goods more often for everyone here."

He nodded. "I know you'd make an awful lot of people happy. Well, if you'll excuse me, I'll let you get back to whatever you were doing. I'm going to go sit at my desk and savor this cheesecake." He held up the cheesecake he had taken a bite out of. "Thanks again for bringing them, Allie."

"You're so welcome, Ben," I said. He closed the door and left, and I turned to Alec. "This place is good for my ego. I love it when people enjoy my baked goods."

"They're fantastic." He leaned back in his chair. "Are there any blueberry cheesecakes at home?"

I nodded. "You know I had to make one for us and another for Lucy."

"Good, I won't steal one of the boxes from the break room, then."

"You better not. You'll have an uprising on your hands," Lucy said.

Lucy and I were getting ready to leave when there was another knock at the door.

"Come in!" Alec called.

When the door opened, I expected to see one of the officers, but it was Bryce Easley. He looked around sheepishly when he realized Lucy and I were there. "I'm sorry. I didn't mean to interrupt anything."

"You're not interrupting a thing," I said. "We just stopped by to visit our favorite detective, and I brought some blueberry cheesecakes for the officers. Would you like one?"

He smiled. "Oh, no thank you. I don't want to take one of the officers' cheesecakes."

"I'll grab one for you," Lucy said in spite of his protest and left to get one from the break room.

"I try to keep everyone happy around here," I said.

"Bryce, come on in," Alec said. "What can I help you with?"

He stepped inside and closed the door behind him. "Like I said, I don't mean to interrupt anything. But I remembered something that I had completely forgotten about. I don't know if it's important, but I thought I had better come down here and talk to you about it."

"If you'd like privacy, I can leave," I offered. I wanted to stay and hear what he had to say, but I didn't want to intrude on the conversation between him and Alec.

The door swung open and Lucy was back with a mini cheesecake and a napkin. "Here you go."

"Thanks, Lucy," he said, taking the cheesecake from her.

"Did you want privacy?" I asked again as Lucy sat down.

He shook his head. "No, that's unnecessary. Really, it might mean nothing at all. But I saw my sister with Jim Martin a couple of days before Christmas. They were standing in front of the coffee shop, talking. I can't believe it slipped my mind, but when Lainey never showed up for Christmas, I just assumed she was mad about something. I never told my parents about seeing her because I didn't want to add to their unhappiness about her not showing up. I thought if I said something, it would just make my dad angrier and hurt my mom even more than she already was."

"Do you remember what day it was that you saw them?" Alec asked, pulling out a small notebook.

He thought about it for a moment, leaning against the door. "I think it must have been the 22nd or the 23rd. Her plane was due to arrive on the 21st. I know it wasn't Christmas Eve because my mom called her that afternoon to ask if she was in town, but she never answered her phone."

"What do you think she was doing with Jim?" I asked. "I thought they broke up in September, and Jim said something about already dating Taylor Jenkins, who he later married, by that time."

"I would think that would have upset Taylor if she knew Jim was talking to Lainey," Lucy said.

I nodded. "I think most women would have an issue with that."

Bryce shrugged. "I don't know what they were talking about. It could have been that they just ran into each other, but I couldn't say for sure. To be honest, it looked like they were having an amicable conversation. Lainey was smiling, which is strange because their breakup was awful. I remember Lainey was very upset with Jim."

"It doesn't make sense that she would be smiling at him then, would it?" Alec asked. "But maybe they had made amends and decided to be friends."

Bryce shrugged. "I guess that could happen, but

why? Lainey wasn't living here in town anymore, and it's not like they had anything that was keeping them in each other's lives. I can't believe I forgot about this. If we had known that she had been murdered right away, I know I would have remembered it and mentioned it to you. But like I said, I just thought she was mad at us and that's why she didn't show up for Christmas. Now that we know she's dead, it makes me wonder about it."

He had a point. Why would they remain in each other's lives, especially since Lainey was glad to be rid of him? Lainey sounded like a young woman who had an unstable personal life, and if the two of them had a nasty breakup, would she have been smiling at him? Stopping to talk to him in front of the coffee shop? It didn't seem likely.

"It's an interesting detail, and I'll keep it in mind," Alec said noncommittally.

Bryce nodded. "I know I already brought up Eli hanging out in that field where Lainey was found, but I also thought I would mention that he was out there again yesterday evening. When I pulled up, he turned around and headed for his truck and just waved at me like nothing was going on."

"I've already talked to Eli," Alec said. "He didn't have much to say."

Bryce straightened up. "Well, I don't mean to take up a lot of your time. I was just driving by the police station and thought I would stop in and talk to you for a minute. I wish I had remembered that detail about seeing Lainey and Dave together at the coffee shop earlier."

"I appreciate you letting me know," Alec said.

He nodded. "You all have a good afternoon. I better get back to the farm. Thanks for the cheesecake."

"You're welcome. It was good seeing you, Bryce," I said as he left. I turned back to Alec. "What do you think?"

"I think I might have another talk with Jim," he said. "There really wouldn't be much reason for Lainey to be happily chatting with him when she came back to visit her family at Christmas time."

"I wonder if Lainey and Jim really broke up that September?" I mused.

"Everybody has said they did," Alec said. "Why?"

I shrugged. "I don't know. Maybe they just argued and then got back together. It would explain who picked her up from the airport, and with her being in

Oregon, Jim was free to date Taylor. Maybe while visiting, Lainey found out that he was seeing someone else and got angry about it."

Lucy turned to me. "That's a good idea. With Lainey being as volatile as she was, she wasn't going to be nice or quiet about it. She was going to make a scene."

"Exactly. And maybe Jim got angry about that, and he killed her." This idea had my mind turning. Whoever killed Lainey was probably close to her, and the friction she and Jim had between them wasn't something new. No, it was something that was ignited over and over in their relationship. And if Lainey found out that Jim was seeing somebody on the side, sparks would fly.

"Maybe," Alec said. "But we don't have any proof leading us in that direction. I'll have to do some more investigating to see what I can come up with."

I nodded. "We'll look into it on our end as well. Somebody else had to have seen her when she came home at Christmas time, especially if she was at the coffee shop."

I had a feeling that would be our key to solving this mystery. Somebody had to have seen her around town.

CHAPTER 15

*B*aking cheesecakes and trying to figure out a murder mystery is time-consuming. I really wanted to find out who killed Lainey, but so far, we were coming up empty-handed. I didn't like that one bit.

The following morning, Lucy and I headed to the Cup and Bean Coffee Shop after our run. I ordered a cherry chocolate muffin with an iced mocha. Lucy went with a slice of pumpkin bread and a vanilla latte.

I eyed her pumpkin bread. "I should have ordered that."

She scooted the pumpkin loaf closer to herself. "You snooze, you lose. You should have thought about that before you ordered the cherry chocolate muffin. But I bet that muffin is delicious, too."

I smiled at my best friend. "I wish fall would get here a little quicker because you know I'm going to be baking and eating all things pumpkin."

She took a sip of her latte. "You won't get any argument from me. I love all things pumpkin too, and I will volunteer to be your taste tester."

We picked up our baked goods and coffees from the counter and headed over to Mr. Winters' table and sat down. Sadie immediately licked my leg, and I rubbed her ear.

"How goes it, ladies?" Mr. Winters asked.

"It goes about as well as it can, I guess," I admitted. "We don't have a suspect for the murder, though. Have you found out anything?"

He shook his head. "No, and it's disappointing. Usually, someone somewhere knows something. Wouldn't you think someone would have seen her when she got into town?"

"That's exactly what we said," Lucy agreed as she broke off a small piece of pumpkin bread and popped it into her mouth. She closed her eyes, held up her thumb and first finger, and gave the A-OK sign.

"Oh, don't tease us," I said. She chuckled. I turned

back to Mr. Winters just as Ellen Allen stormed over to our table.

"Allie, when is your husband going to make an arrest in my cousin's murder?"

I shook my head. "Ellen, he's doing all he can to find her killer. You just have to be patient."

She took a deep breath. "Well, she's haunting me from the dead, and I can't take it anymore."

"What?" Lucy asked incredulously.

"What are you talking about?" I asked.

She put her hands on her hips. "Just what I said. Lainey is haunting me from the dead because her killer hasn't been found. I'm not going to get any sleep until they're behind bars. Tell your husband to hurry."

I knew Ellen was a little nutty, but this took the cake. "Exactly what do you mean by your cousin is haunting you?"

"She keeps calling me," she said, emphasizing the word 'calling'.

"What does she say?" I asked.

She shook her head. "She doesn't say anything. That's just it. She's dead. I know she wants her killer found, and I know she isn't going to give me any rest until they're put behind bars."

"That sounds crazy to me," Mr. Winters said and took a sip of his black coffee.

"How do you know it's her if she doesn't say anything?" I asked.

She threw her arms in the air. "How do you think I know? It's her phone number!"

I was shocked to hear this. "Really? Someone's calling you from her phone number?"

Before she could answer, Bryce walked up to the table. "Cuz, how are you doing?" He reached out to hug her, but Ellen remained rigid.

"I'm doing terrible! Lainey is haunting me! She keeps calling me every night. If her killer isn't found soon, I'm going to lose my mind." She shook her head.

Bryce's eyes widened. "What do you mean, she's calling you?"

She shook her head again. "I mean, she's calling me. Her phone number is on the display on my phone, but she never says a word." She turned back to me. "Allie, I'm begging you, make your husband find her killer."

"Ellen, I'm sorry you're having trouble, but Alec is doing everything he can to find her killer. Maybe someone found her phone and is calling you because Lainey programmed your number into her phone."

Lucy turned to me and mouthed the word 'wow'.

"Ellen, Lainey is not calling you. That isn't even possible," Bryce assured her. "Maybe they've already given away her phone number to somebody else, and they don't understand that they're calling the wrong number."

"That's a possibility, too," I said.

Ellen seemed to consider this, then shook her head. "No. It's Lainey. I know it is."

"Ellen, I promise you that Alec is doing everything he can to find her killer. I'll let him know that somebody is calling you from her phone number." It seemed like an awful big coincidence that somebody with the same phone number as Ellen's recently murdered cousin was calling her. I didn't buy it for a minute. This wasn't some random happening.

"Don't let it upset you," Bryce said. "I'm sure the cops are going to find Lainey's killer soon. Then we can all rest easy."

She took a sip of her coffee, her eyes on me. "Allie, I'm holding you to it. Find Lainey's killer."

I didn't know what else to say to reassure her. The police were doing everything possible to find the culprit.

Bryce scowled. "That makes me angry that somebody is tormenting you, Ellen. They have no right to do this to you. Allie, we need Lainey's killer found. It takes a lot of nerve to torment Lainey's family that way."

"You think it's the killer?" Lucy asked.

He shrugged. "Who else could it be? I don't know. Maybe I'm wrong, but maybe they are doing it just because they think it's funny. Some people are just horrible monsters."

"I'm so sorry," I said. "I know this has to be so difficult for you, Ellen. It makes me angry, too."

"Thanks, Allie. I just need it to stop." She reached over and hugged Bryce. "I've got to go now. I've got to be at work in ten minutes."

"Call me later when you get home," Bryce said. "We'll talk."

She nodded and headed out. Bryce turned back to us. "Wow. That's crazy."

"I'll say," Mr. Winters said. "I wonder what's going on there?"

"Bryce, how are you doing?" I wondered if he was taking enough time to grieve for his sister after I spoke to Jason the other day. Working through it wasn't a bad idea, but I hoped he was taking some time to grieve.

He took a deep breath. "Well, I guess I'm doing better than Ellen is. But I'm still trying to take this thing day by day. We had a little excitement at the farm yesterday."

"Oh?" I was all ears.

He nodded. "Our farm manager, Dave Evans, and Eli Thompson got into an argument over Lainey's murder. Eli quit and walked off the job."

I was shocked to hear this. "Are you serious? After all those years, Eli just quits?"

"That must have been some argument," Lucy said.

He nodded. "Dave said that Eli made a smart remark about Lainey's body being out there in the blueberry bushes. I'm not even going to repeat what he said—it was so awful. Then Dave yelled at him and told him he should be ashamed of himself, but Eli just laughed. By the time I got there, I thought they were going to punch each other."

"That doesn't sound like something Eli would do," I said. "Did you talk to him?"

He shook his head. "No, I'm so angry about what Dave said that I don't want to see Eli ever again. He wouldn't have walked off the job if it wasn't true."

"Well, what if he didn't really say it?" Mr. Winters asked. "I know Eli, and he's a good guy. He wouldn't say anything inappropriate, at least not on purpose."

"I know Dave well enough to know that he wouldn't lie," Bryce said.

I couldn't imagine Eli behaving that way. "What did your father say about it?"

He shook his head. "Oh, he's angry about it. He can't believe Eli would just say something like that, and he said that if Eli hadn't quit, he would have fired him."

"But that's so sad. He worked on that farm for so many years. He always spoke well of your grandparents and your family," I pointed out. "I just can't believe he would do something like that."

Bryce pressed his lips together for a moment. "I think he killed Lainey. I told you he was hanging out in that field, and I think it was because he was worried about somebody finding her body. Now it's out in the open and he's worried about getting caught."

"But I tripped over her," I said. "If he had been out there, why wouldn't he have covered her better?"

He shrugged, glancing away. "I don't know, but I swear he's the killer."

I didn't feel like this made any sense, and I was

worried about Eli. He was going to try to wait a couple more years to retire. Since this was a spur-of-the-moment decision, I wondered if he had money to take care of himself until he could figure out what he was going to do.

Lucy shook her head. "I don't think Eli could hurt a fly. He's one of the sweetest people in this town. He's a hard worker, and he's been very loyal to you and your family. You and your father need to speak to him and see what he has to say about the argument."

"I agree," I said. "Something doesn't add up because it just isn't in Eli's nature to do something like that."

Bryce glanced at the short line at the front counter, then turned back. "Yeah, I know. You're right. We need to have a talk with him. I'll talk to my dad about it. I hate to lose a good employee like Eli, but we will not put up with that kind of behavior if he did do it."

I nodded, feeling relieved. There had to have been some sort of misunderstanding between Eli and Dave. Or Dave was making this up because he was hiding something.

CHAPTER 16

*I*t was later that evening when I had just finished telling Alec everything that had happened at the coffee shop when our doorbell rang.

"I wonder who that could be?" he sighed. "I was hoping we could relax for a few minutes." He headed to the front door. He had just gotten off work, and I knew he was tired.

I followed him to see who it might be and was surprised to see Grace Easley standing on our doorstep.

"Good evening, Grace," Alec said.

She nodded. "Good evening, Alec, Allie. I hate to disturb you both," she said, glancing over her shoulder and then turning back to us. "But I've had a hard time trying to come to terms with what happened to my daughter. So I made some pumpkin bread today to take my mind off things." She held up a plate wrapped in plastic wrap. "You're always baking for everyone else, Allie, so I thought I would bring some by. Do you like pumpkin bread?"

"Are you kidding me?" I said. "It's like you read my mind. I've had pumpkin spice on my mind for days now, and fall can't get here soon enough. Would you like to come in? We can have some coffee and a slice of pumpkin bread."

"I love pumpkin bread," Alec said.

She smiled. "I would love to come in. That is if I'm not disturbing you."

I shook my head and opened the door wider. "No, you're not disturbing us. Let's go to the kitchen, and I'll get the coffee."

We headed to the kitchen, closing the door behind us.

"I know it won't be as good as anything you would make," she said.

I looked over my shoulder. "What? I bet it's delicious. I'm so excited that you thought of us and brought us some pumpkin bread. Lucy ordered some at the coffee shop this morning and I really wished I had gotten some too. I'm crazy about anything pumpkin."

She nodded, and we went to the kitchen table where I offered her a seat, then went to the coffee pot. I had just made a fresh pot right before Alec got home. Although the caffeine wasn't great for me at this hour, I love to sit and enjoy a cup in the late afternoons or evenings. "It will just take me a second."

Alec went to the cupboards and got three coffee cups along with dessert plates, and brought them to the table. "How are you doing, Grace?"

She nodded. "I guess I'm doing as well as I can be. Honestly, I just keep thinking that Lainey will call me, and we'll sit and talk just like we used to." She took a deep breath and let it out slowly.

I brought the coffee pot to the table while Alec got some cream and sugar. "I can't say it enough. That's the worst part of losing someone. Expecting the phone call you'll never get."

She nodded. "You're exactly right."

I unwrapped the pumpkin bread, and the scent of cinnamon and allspice wafted towards me. I inhaled deeply. "Oh, that smells so good. I can hardly wait."

She smiled. "I add a little extra spice. I hope it's not too much."

"I do the same. It's going to be delicious." I cut three slices of pumpkin bread while Alec poured the coffee, and we sat down.

"What's on your mind, Grace?" Alec asked as he stirred sugar into his coffee.

Grace flinched as she poured cream into her cup. Her eyes darted from me to Alec and then back. "I figured out what that key was for—the one that was in Lainey's pocket."

"Oh?" Alec said with interest as he pushed the sugar bowl toward her and took the cream she offered. "What does it belong to?"

"It belongs to a small storage bin. I had completely forgotten about it, but then it occurred to me that before she moved to Oregon, she had rented it because her apartment was very tiny, and she had too many things. She asked me to pack her things up and send them to her when she found a place that was large enough, but she never let me know whether she had. I hadn't realized that the payment for the storage shed was still coming out of my husband's checking account. He never balances it; he just throws more money into it when it gets low."

"And did you find something of interest in the storage shed?" Alec asked.

She cut into her pumpkin bread with the corner of her fork before answering. "Mostly it was clothes and shoes, with a few books, and some things from her high school years. It wasn't very much stuff, but the closet space in that tiny apartment was unbelievably small, so she didn't have room for it. But I found her journal."

I stared at her, holding my breath. "There was something in it?"

She nodded and put her fork down without eating the pumpkin bread. She dug into her purse, pulling out a yellow and pink floral journal. "She wrote about her relationship with Jim. If she were still alive, I would feel so bad about reading it, but I felt like I needed to. I miss her so much, and I just wanted to hear her words, even if they weren't audible if that makes any sense."

I nodded. "It makes perfect sense." I cut into my pumpkin bread and took a bite. It was the perfect balance of cloves, all spice, and cinnamon and tasted divine. "Oh Grace, this is delicious. It's so moist, and the spice balance is perfect."

She smiled. "That means a lot coming from you."

I nodded. "Thank you. I appreciate hearing that from you, too."

She sobered and turned to Alec. "She said Dave grabbed her around the throat and slammed her into a wall during an argument."

I gasped. "Oh no."

Alec took the journal from her. "When did that happen?"

"It was September 8th, the year before last. It makes me sick to read those words. She said she was afraid of him, and that she had to break it off because she didn't know what else he might do to her."

Alec flipped through the journal and found the entry, reading in silence. I took a sip of my coffee, trying to think of something to say, but what do you say to a mother who just discovered that her daughter was being abused and then had been murdered?

When Alec had read several pages, he looked up at her. "Can I keep this?"

"Certainly. He's her killer, isn't he? Jim killed her."

Alec was quiet for a moment before answering. "I'm going to have another talk with him, and I'll confront him with this. Please don't say anything to him before then. We don't know that he's her killer, but this is damning evidence."

She nodded, not looking at either of us. "That's

what I thought." With trembling hands, she lifted her coffee cup to her lips and took a sip.

"Grace, Bryce told us what happened between Eli and Dave." I wanted to find out what she thought about the situation.

She looked up at me with tears in her eyes. "Yes, I'm afraid things have been quite chaotic around the farm lately. Really, I guess it's been that way for a while, but I never would have thought that Eli would just quit and walk off the job like that."

"Bryce said that Eli said something awful to Dave." I took another bite of the pumpkin bread. It was perfect.

"I don't believe for one minute Eli said anything as awful as what Dave claimed. Eli has been a faithful employee and an extended member of our family. I think of him as a cousin of sorts. And if you want to know my opinion, I think Dave lied."

"Why would he do that?" Alec asked, looking up from his coffee.

"Because he and Eli never got along. I don't like Dave, although I rarely express my opinion about my husband's employees. I figure he's more hands-on with the farm, and he knows what he's doing. But I don't know what he sees in Dave. I think Dave lies, and I think he treats the employees badly. I wish he would have fired him years ago."

"Has he given your husband a reason to fire him?" I asked.

She nodded. "Yes, he's always stirring up trouble with the employees. About eight years ago, we had a nice young man who was a diligent, hard worker, but Dave didn't like him. Dave fired him without permission, and although Frank was livid about it, he didn't do anything about it."

"So he feels he can do whatever he wants?" Alec asked.

She nodded. "Yes, he does. I'm sure he knows I don't care for him because he's always trying to be charming toward me when I see him around the farm. But I'm not buying his act for one minute. It makes me sick that Eli quit the way he did."

"Do you think he would come back if you asked him?" I asked.

She looked at me and sighed. "I already have, and he said he wouldn't come back. He said he'd been mulling over retirement anyway, and this just inspired him to do it. I told him to file his unemployment claim, and I would sign it saying we laid him off. I also wrote him a severance check. Frank had a fit when he found out, but I don't care. You don't turn your back on loyal employees, and you don't turn your back on people you consider to be family."

Tears sprang to my eyes at this. "Grace, you're a good person."

She shook her head. "We didn't deserve an employee as good as Eli, and I will not allow him to be hurt in any way because he felt the need to leave without notice."

My estimation of Grace as a woman, and as a human being, rose in that moment. I had always liked her and thought well of her, but this brought it to a whole new level.

CHAPTER 17

*W*hen Lucy and I finished our morning run, we stopped by the flower shop to pick up some yellow daisies for her grandmother's grave. Grandma Opal had lived to be ninety, and Lucy never forgot to put a bouquet of yellow daisies on her grave on her birthday.

"I'm so sorry," I said as she placed the flowers in the receptacle near the headstone. She had also brought a small pink bunny to add to the arrangement.

She knelt down and gazed at the headstone lovingly. "She was a tiny force to be reckoned with. She loved life, and she was the happiest person I ever met."

"I bet she was a lot of fun when you were little," I said gently. I had accompanied Lucy many times over the years to place the yellow daisies on her grandmother's grave and never tired of hearing Lucy's stories about her life.

"She would have been one hundred and twenty today. I wish she were still here to see all the great-grandchildren and great-great-grandchildren. She loved the babies."

I smiled. "That's how a grandmother should be. She should love all the babies that come into the family and make sure they know it."

She smiled with tears in her eyes. "I miss her, but I know she's well now, and she isn't in pain anymore, and that's what gets us all through."

"I know."

We headed back to the car. Grandma Opal had arthritis in nearly every joint of her body when she passed, but she had still been smiling through it all.

"Hey, look there," she said, tipping her head in the direction just past the car. I followed her gaze and saw Bryce walking slowly toward a freshly dug grave.

"Let's go say hello," I said. We hurried past my car and headed toward it. The funeral had been two days earlier, so there was no headstone yet.

"Hello, Bryce," I greeted him.

He looked over his shoulder and seemed surprised to see us. He held a small bouquet of flowers in his hand. "Oh, I didn't see you two there. Good morning."

I nodded as we walked over to where he stood. "Those flowers are beautiful."

He glanced down at the bouquet in his hand. "Yeah, I picked out a bunch with lots of pinks and purples because I know she would have loved them."

"That's sweet of you," Lucy said. "I just brought yellow daisies for my grandmother. They were her favorite flower."

"I feel like it's the least I could do." He smiled sadly. "It still doesn't seem real. I guess it'll be a while before it really hits."

"I'm sorry about all of this. How is your mom doing?" I asked.

He nodded, still holding the flowers. "She's doing as well as she can, I guess. Honestly, I told her that not a lot was going to change in the family because we rarely saw Lainey anymore. Maybe I shouldn't have, but it's the truth."

That seemed like an odd thing to say, considering his sister had just been murdered. "How did she react to that?"

His eyes met mine. "I guess it was the wrong thing to say, but what I meant was, we didn't see her every day anymore and hadn't for a long time. I didn't mean it in a bad way."

I nodded. "It's still difficult for all of you, I know."

"Yeah, it is. My sister and Jason were closer than I was to her. He's going to miss her an awful lot."

"I know he will," I said. "I've got to make a blueberry cheesecake and bring it to him. I ran into him at the store last week, and I told him I would, but I just haven't gotten around to it yet."

"That's nice," Bryce said, forcing himself to smile.

"Bryce, how have things been since Eli quit?" I asked. "He was at the farm for so long. I'm sure it's going to be hard adjusting without him."

He shrugged. "Eli and I didn't see eye to eye on a lot of things, and to be honest, it might be good for everyone that he's gone now."

"What do you mean?" Lucy asked.

"Exactly what I said. Eli was trouble. And I suspect he is responsible for my sister's death. His behavior was suspicious, hanging out in that field where her body was found. If he was innocent, why didn't he see her and report it? I've been thinking about it nonstop, so I went to his house yesterday and asked him if he killed Lainey. He denied it, but I know he did it."

"You have a point about why he didn't see her body in the field while he was out there," I said carefully. "Do you think he murdered her?"

He nodded. "You bet I do. He'll probably never tell the truth about it, so I don't know if we'll ever get a conviction. He had the nerve to say that if he did it, they would never find the evidence to convict him because he would have been smart enough to destroy it."

"He came right out and said that?" Lucy asked.

He nodded. "He sure did. I can't stand it. I can't stand the fact that he's free to do whatever he wants while my sister is right here in this grave." He pointed at the mound of dirt as he spoke.

"I have a hard time thinking of Eli as a killer," I said. "He just doesn't seem the type." Did Eli really say that? It didn't seem possible that he would behave that way.

He frowned. "That's just what he wants you to believe. He's not a nice person at all, and he has a lot of secrets. A lot of them."

"But what would be his reason for killing her?" Lucy asked.

The cellophane around the bouquet of flowers crackled as he tightened his grip on it. "Honestly, I don't have an answer to that yet. I think Eli had a secret, and Lainey discovered it. He had to kill her so she wouldn't tell anyone."

What Bryce was saying didn't make sense. What could Lainey have discovered about Eli? "I'm not sure what you're trying to get at. What kind of secret could Eli have that Lainey could have discovered?"

He looked away for a moment, staring at the grave. "I don't know what kind of secret it is. But you have to understand that my grandfather hired people who needed a second chance. Criminals. Drug addicts. Alcoholics. He didn't hire the best of the best, and I know Eli was one of those people my grandfather wanted to give a second chance to. Whenever we ask about his family, he's always vague. He won't tell us where he lived before he came to Sandy Harbor. He claims he has no family left."

"Why do you find that strange?" I asked. "There are plenty of people in this world whose families have passed away." Maybe I felt a little protective of Eli because I liked him so much, but it sounded like Bryce was looking for reasons not to like Eli.

"Because I think he's an ex-con whom my grandfather gave a second chance to. My grandfather was a soft touch. And I think Eli is keeping his past a secret because he committed some awful crime. Maybe Lainey discovered it and blackmailed him. She wasn't above doing something like that, you know. People try to paint her as this sweet angel, but those who really knew her know better." He squeezed the flowers tighter.

"Why do you think this is true, though?" I asked. "Do you have any solid proof that she did something like this?"

"You think she was holding this secret over Eli's head?" Lucy asked.

He stared at the grave and licked his lips. "I caught Eli and Lainey speaking harshly to one another a couple of years ago, shortly before she left. I didn't hear what it was about, but when I asked them both privately what was going on, neither of them would say. I've been thinking it over, and I think Lainey discovered Eli's secret and threatened to tell my dad. My dad never really cared for Eli. The only reason he kept him on as long as he did was because my grandfather thought so highly of Eli."

"If your grandfather thought so highly of him, shouldn't that be enough?" I asked.

He sighed and turned away, kneeling down by the grave and laying the bouquet of flowers on top. The little canister with water wasn't there yet, so those flowers were going to dry out quickly. "You don't know Eli like I do. He would do anything to keep his secrets to himself." He stood up and turned back to us. "It's been nice talking to you, ladies. I've got to get back to the farm and get to work. There's always so much work to do on the farm."

I nodded. "I'm sure there is. See you later, Bryce."

We watched as he walked back to his truck, and then I turned to Lucy. "What do you think about that?"

She shook her head and glanced at Bryce's truck as he started it. "I don't know what to think, but I can't see Eli being a criminal."

I nodded as we headed back to my car. I hoped what Bryce said about Eli wasn't true, but I realized I didn't know him well enough to know if it was.

CHAPTER 18

"Where are we going?" Lucy asked as I made a left-hand turn out of the cemetery.

"To talk to Eli."

She looked at me as I drove. "Why? Do you really think he would tell you his secrets?"

I shrugged. "I don't know if he'll tell me his secrets. Honestly, the only secret I care about is who killed Lainey Easley. If that's the secret he's keeping, I want to know about it. He can keep the other ones to himself." It wasn't my business to know about Eli's past. Unless he was willing to share it, that is.

I gripped the steering wheel as I drove, not wanting to believe that Eli could have murdered someone. But one thing I knew was that Clem Easley was a big-hearted man. I had often heard that he gave lots of people second chances by offering them jobs at the blueberry farm. Maybe Eli was one of those people, and maybe he was harboring a huge secret.

We pulled up to Eli's house, and I parked the car. He lived in a tiny house that couldn't have been over five or six hundred square feet. The yard was immaculately kept, but the house desperately needed a fresh coat of paint.

"I don't see a car. I wonder if he's home?" Lucy asked.

I shook my head. "Let's find out." There was no garage attached to the house, and no car in sight, so Eli may not have been there. I knocked on the door, and we waited, but no one came. I knocked again, louder this time. The house was so small; there was no way he couldn't hear me if he was home. A minute later, I heard footsteps inside. The door opened, and Eli looked surprised to see us. "Well, how are you, ladies?"

I smiled. "We're great, Eli. How about you? We heard you left your job. Are you enjoying retirement?"

He laughed. "I'm not sure I know how to do that.

When you've worked as many years as I have, it doesn't seem right not to have someplace to go. I guess I'll have to try to adjust by going fishing or something."

"I think that's a swell way to spend your retirement," Lucy said. "Or you could volunteer somewhere. Doing things for others is a great way to spend your time."

He blinked. "I never thought about that. Maybe I'll have to check around and see if I can find somewhere to volunteer."

"Volunteer work makes you feel like you're a part of something bigger than yourself," I said. "Eli, why did you quit your job at the farm?"

He shook his head. "I decided I had had enough of Dave and Bryce. I never really even cared much for Frank if you want to know the truth."

"Oh, I didn't realize that," I said. "I guess I don't know Frank that well."

He nodded. "Frank is nothing like his father, I can tell you that. Clem was a good, decent man."

That statement made me wonder if Frank wasn't a good, decent man, then what was he? "Eli, why didn't you tell my husband everything you told us? He needs to know everything so he can talk to the right people and figure out who killed Lainey."

He pressed his lips together and shook his head. "Because it wasn't my business. I never should have said anything to you two. You shouldn't have told your husband."

"I'm sorry if you thought you told me that in confidence. But if he needs to talk to somebody, he needs all the information available. If Dave is behaving suspiciously, don't you want Alec to speak to him about the murder?" I asked.

He leaned on the doorframe, making no effort to invite us in. "Yeah, I want Lainey's killer found. But I don't want the wrong person arrested, so why should I be talking about something that I don't know enough about? It would be terrible if the wrong person was arrested for her murder."

I sighed, deciding on a different tack. "Eli, how did you and Clem Easley meet?"

He shrugged. "I needed a job, so I stopped by the blueberry farm and talked to him. He hired me on the spot. That doesn't happen these days, I can tell you that."

"Where did you work before the blueberry farm?"

Lucy asked, catching on to my new line of questioning.

His brow wrinkled. "What difference does it make?"

She shrugged. "I just wondered, is all."

He frowned. "I don't talk about my former life. There's nothing to talk about. They always bugged me at the farm, asking questions about my family and stuff. What difference does it make? It didn't effect the job I did there, so why ask about it? Clem didn't pry."

I shook my head. "You're right. It's none of their business. It's not like you have to tell them. And it's none of ours." I gazed at him, hoping he would tell me something anyway.

He closed his eyes for a moment. "Let's just say that I made some mistakes. Some of those mistakes I'm still paying for. I have a daughter who doesn't like to acknowledge that I'm her father."

"I'm sorry," I said. "That must be very painful for you."

"That's tough," Lucy said.

He nodded. "But I could never tell anybody at the farm who she was because I was afraid I would lose my job."

"What do you mean?" I asked. "What difference would it have made if they knew about your daughter?"

He gazed at her, then turned to me. "I guess it doesn't matter now since I don't work there anymore. But I had an affair with Frank's cousin's wife, and we had a daughter together."

I stood there, trying to figure out who he was talking about, but I didn't have a clue. "Who?" I finally asked.

"Anne Marie Cauthy."

Lucy and I gasped in unison.

"What?" Lucy asked.

"What?" I asked. "You had an affair with Anne Marie Cauthy?" And then I realized who his daughter was. "Ellen Allen? Ellen Allen is your daughter?"

My mind was spinning. Never in a million years would I have thought that Ellen had a wonderful father like Eli since she was anything but wonderful. And he was saying that she didn't want to acknowledge *him*?

He smiled. "Yes. But Anne Marie was married to Bill, who is Frank's cousin, and if Frank found out about it, I would have lost my job because he and Bill are close."

"Oh," Lucy said, drawing the word out.

"Eli, it's your business what you do in your personal life, and I can see why you would want to keep that from them," I said. "But why were you in the field where Lainey's body was found?"

His brow furrowed. "I wasn't in that field where her body was found."

"You weren't?" I asked. "But several people have said that you were. Alec said you told him you went to check the blueberries there."

He shook his head. "No, I was in some nearby fields because I got better reception out there and because I didn't want anybody to overhear the phone calls I made to Ellen. She's very demanding and would text me multiple times throughout the day sometimes asking me to call her. I did check blueberries nearby, but I never went to the area Lainey's body was." He thought about it for a moment and then laughed. "Oh, you know what? When I finished my phone calls, I cut across the blueberry fields and went through the one where Lainey was buried. But I never saw her because I never really stopped to look around in that field. I was just passing through."

"So somebody just saw you cutting through the field and thought you were hanging around there doing something you shouldn't be." The body had become uncovered, but it might not have been until recently, so I believed him when he said he never saw it.

"That makes sense," Lucy said. "But it doesn't make sense that Ellen Allen is your daughter. She's not the nicest person around, you know. No offense."

He chuckled. "Yes, I know. She didn't know I was her father until about fifteen years ago. By then she was a senior in high school, and her personality had already developed. I blame Bill for that. She acts just like him. But ever since we figured out she was my daughter, she's been asking me for money." He rolled his eyes. "All she has to do is look around this place to know I don't have much money."

Lucy scowled. "That sounds just like Ellen. I worked with her at the flower shop a few years ago, and she was the most incompetent, foul-mouthed, hateful person I've ever worked with." Her eyes widened. "Oh, I'm so sorry. I shouldn't talk about your daughter that way."

Eli laughed. "I can't argue with you about any of that. It's the truth, but I love her anyway. She's my daughter. But I don't have much extra money to give her like she wants, and that doesn't make her happy. But she'll just have to get over it."

I sighed. "Eli, I'm so glad you didn't murder Lainey Easley. You didn't, right?"

He shook his head. "No, I didn't murder her or anybody else. I sure hope your husband finds her killer, and I'm betting he'll find them somewhere on that farm."

I didn't doubt that the killer was probably on the farm. And I was relieved that it wasn't Eli.

CHAPTER 19

"*A*re you going to make any more cheesecake?" Lucy asked as I drove. She was holding two blueberry cheesecakes on her lap. One of them was for Grace and Frank, and the other was for Jason. I could have made one for Bryce, but when I mentioned bringing one to Jason, Bryce gave no indication that he might like to have one. I could have made it anyway, but I was low on cream cheese and didn't feel like making a run to the grocery store.

"Don't tell me you and Ed have already worked your way through that second cheesecake." I glanced at her.

"Okay, I won't tell you."

I chuckled. "If you would like another cheesecake,

164

I'll pick up some more cream cheese the next time I go to the grocery store, and I'll make you one. I'm out of blueberries, though, so it might be a different flavor."

She looked at me, one eyebrow raised. "We bought an awful lot of blueberries. How could you be out of them already?"

I shrugged. "I've been making blueberry smoothies, blueberry protein shakes, and Alec and I have been eating them fresh. I guess I could pick some up while we're here at the farm, though."

She sighed. "I suppose I don't need more cheesecake. We've skipped too many of our runs, and I can tell by the way my clothes fit that I've eaten too much cheesecake."

She wasn't wrong. We had gone on a few runs, but we had gotten out of the habit of our almost daily runs, and we needed to get back to it. Otherwise, my running clothes would have to be replaced with a larger size. If you're going to bake, you've got to figure out how to keep all that deliciousness from going to your waist.

"Starting Monday, let's get back on our regular running routine. I miss it."

"I do too. It wasn't that long ago that I thought I

would never be able to say that I miss running, but I do," she said.

"It has an addictive element to it, doesn't it?"

She nodded as I parked at the blueberry farm. "It really does. I've been trying to get Ed to come along with us, but he keeps making excuses. Apparently, he has to work." She rolled her eyes.

I laughed again. "There's something to be said about being able to make the mortgage payment."

We got out of the car, and I took one of the cheesecakes from her. I hoped Jason and his mother would be home; otherwise, we would have to take these home and try again tomorrow.

I went up the steps to Grace's house and knocked on the door. When no one answered, I tried again.

"Maybe she isn't home," Lucy said when there was still no answer.

I nodded. "Let's go try Jason's house. We can leave both cheesecakes there if he's home." We headed around the back of the house. They were cute little white clapboard houses with dark green shutters.

We went up the porch steps of the smallest, and just before I raised my hand to knock on the door, I heard voices coming from inside.

"I know what you did! I hate you!"

I turned to look at Lucy, and her eyes were wide.

"Do you think I care what you were both up to, sweet-talking Mom and Dad that way? You both thought you were going to take over the farm, but believe me, it won't happen. Not on my watch."

"I don't know what you're talking about," the first voice said. "Just get out of here!"

"I don't think I'll be doing that. Not now."

"What are you doing? Have you lost your mind?"

"I haven't lost my mind, and I'm not going to lose the farm, either. It's mine. It belongs to me."

"It belongs to the family."

I glanced back over my shoulder, but there was no one nearby.

"What do we do?" Lucy whispered.

I didn't know what to do.

"Get up!"

"What are you doing? Get out of here! I knew you killed Lainey. You couldn't stand her from the day she was born."

Lucy and I looked at each other and gasped.

"It doesn't matter what I did, because you're not going to be around long enough to tell anybody. Get in the bedroom."

"Come on. You can't mean this. I won't tell anyone."

There was a scuffling sound that came from inside, and someone grunted.

Without thinking, I reached for the doorknob and turned it slowly. It gave way. When I slowly pushed the door open, I saw Jason sitting on the couch with his back toward us, and Bryce standing over him with a small pistol in his hand. Before I could think about it and chicken out, I took the bakery box with the blueberry cheesecake in it and hurled it at Bryce. He looked up, but it was too late as the cheesecake hit him square in the face. With a shout of surprise, he backpedaled and tripped over an ottoman, landing on his back with a grunt.

Jason looked back at us in shock and then launched himself at his brother.

"Get off me!" Bryce shouted.

"You're not going to get away with killing Lainey!" They struggled as the gun flew from Bryce's hand, clattering on the floor. I hurried around the side of the couch, with Lucy following close behind. To get to the gun, I was going to have to step over Jason and Bryce. Jason was straddling Bryce, trying to hold him down and reach for the gun at the same time. He looked up at me desperately. "Help me!"

I was going to have to do it. I stepped over Jason's legs, but Bryce kicked me just as I was moving across him, and I fell to the floor with a thud. I let out a yelp, and I heard Lucy talking to the 911 operator. Good. If we could get the gun away from Bryce, the police would be here soon.

Bryce punched me in the shoulder as I reached for the gun, and I screamed again.

Jason punched him in the face, and Bryce grunted. "Don't hit a woman!" Jason shouted.

I reached with my good arm and grabbed the gun. Then I rolled over and sat up, holding the gun on Bryce. "Move, Bryce!"

He stopped and looked at me, his eyes going wide. "What are you doing, Allie? Jason killed my sister. You need to point the gun at him."

I shook my head, holding the gun with both hands. "I heard everything. You're the one who killed Lainey."

He shook his head, his eyes wide. "No, it was Jason. He's the murderer. Don't let him have that gun."

Jason straightened up and held his hand out for

the gun, breathing hard. "Thanks, Allie. I'll take it from here."

That was when I realized that not only did Bryce and Jason look a lot alike, but their voices sounded very similar. What *had* I heard? I wanted to look at Lucy, but she was still on the phone with 911, and I didn't dare take my eyes off the two brothers.

"Don't give it to him," Bryce begged. "He'll kill us all."

I glanced at Jason. "He's lying," he assured me. "Give me the gun." There was a pleading in his voice, but I didn't trust it. Was I confused about what just happened?

I carefully got to my feet, the gun still trained on the two of them. "I think I'll just hold on to the gun until the police get here if that's all right with the two of you." My shoulder throbbed where Bryce had hit me. Or was it Jason who had hit me? I had been concentrating on the gun and had only seen a fist reach out and hit me. They were both wearing white T-shirts and blue jeans. Had it been Bryce? I wasn't even sure.

"Allie, it's fine," Jason assured me, still breathing hard. "I won't let him hurt you. Give me the gun."

I took a deep breath. I wanted to back away, but I

was trapped. There was a loveseat behind me, and it was against the wall. "Both of you get up and move back."

"You can't think that I killed my sister, can you?" Jason asked.

"I don't know, but the police will sort it out when they get here."

Jason got off Bryce and stood up, but he wouldn't back up. "Come on, Allie. Give me the gun."

I shook my head. "I said back up," I said through clenched teeth.

"Don't let him have that gun," Bryce said. "Please, Allie, don't let him have it."

Jason took a step closer. "Give me the gun, Allie."

"I'm warning you, Jason. You have to get back. Both of you go stand against that wall over there." I nodded at the wall behind them.

"I want the gun," Jason said firmly. "Bryce admitted to killing Lainey, and he will not get away with it."

"You're not going to get the gun. And if you don't back up and stand against that wall, I'm going to shoot you," I said. I may have sounded resolute, but I was shaking inside. I needed Alec to come and take care of this situation.

Bryce suddenly lunged for the gun, but at that moment, another pink bakery box flew across the room and hit him in the side of the head. He gave a grunt of pain and tripped over his own feet, hitting the recliner. I jumped onto the couch and climbed over the back of it to stand with Lucy. "If either of you moves, I'm going to shoot you."

I stood with the gun trained on them while Bryce swore under his breath.

"I really hated to ruin that cheesecake," Lucy whispered.

I nodded. "I'll make you another for saving me."

"Oh good," she said.

CHAPTER 20

"*T*hat looks delicious," Lucy said as I put the finishing touches on the cheesecake.

Alec had shown up with the other officers and arrested both brothers, taking them downtown for questioning. Since I knew Alec wouldn't be home for a while, we stopped by the grocery store to pick up ingredients for cheesecake, and I grabbed a box of blueberries from the farm before we left. Literally. I suppose it was stealing, but I could take the money to Grace another day. I was glad she wasn't there to witness her sons being arrested.

"I'm suddenly starving," I said. "I'll text Alec in a bit and see if he's coming home soon. If he isn't, I'm cutting into this cheesecake."

Ed came over and leaned over the kitchen counter. "That cheesecake looks divine. And of course, I already know it tastes divine because we've had it before."

I looked up at him. "Ed, Lucy saved my life today."

Lucy shook her head. "That's not true. I'm sure you would have kept hold of that gun if I hadn't thrown the cheesecake."

"Maybe, or maybe not. Bryce is bigger than me, and I could have been in a lot of trouble if you hadn't been there."

"I knew I married you for a reason," Ed said, nodding at Lucy. "You're a good woman, Lucy."

She chuckled. "Thanks, Honey."

I smiled as I heard the key in the lock. "Oh, let me get some coffee brewing."

I went to the coffee maker and measured out ground coffee.

"What's going on in here?" Alec asked, walking into the kitchen.

"Allie made us a blueberry cheesecake," Ed informed him. "We can't get enough of it."

"I'm also making some coffee so we can all have some cheesecake and coffee," I said setting the canister of coffee down and grabbing the water pitcher. "Give me just a minute, and I'll get this done. Then you can tell us what happened."

Alec came up behind me, wrapped his arms around me, and kissed my neck. "Why do you keep putting yourself in harm's way?"

I shook my head. "I don't know. It's just a habit I've picked up somewhere."

Ed laughed. "And now she's got this one doing it, too." He tipped his head at Lucy.

"Oh, you," Lucy said, patting Ed's arm.

Alec sighed. "They're incorrigible, Ed. Simply incorrigible."

"True, true," Ed agreed, shaking his head.

"Lucy, please take the cheesecake to the table and get some plates. I'll take care of the coffee." We were in a hurry to hear the details, so I placed a cup under the flow of coffee. Forget about the pot.

Within a few minutes, we had coffee made with cream and sugar on the table, and the cheesecake ready.

Lucy cut into the cheesecake, giving us each a generous slice.

I turned to Alec. "So, what happened? We couldn't tell by the voices who was who. Or at least we thought we knew, but then Bryce confused me."

"Jason was suspicious that Bryce killed Lainey because he kept pressing the point that Eli had to be Lainey's killer. Jason couldn't imagine Eli doing it and Bryce wouldn't let up about it." He stirred sugar into his coffee. "Bryce killed Lainey. He was afraid she was returning to the farm and wanted to rejoin the family. He said she was his mother's favorite and thought she would be put in charge of things and he couldn't bear that. He also found out that Lainey was still in the will. He had assumed that since she wanted nothing to do with the farm, she would be cut out of it."

I took a plate with a slice of cheesecake from Lucy. "Why did he think Lainey would take over? He was the one working on the farm, and Frank said he loved it."

"That's just it. He loved the farm, and he was afraid of losing it. Lainey was demanding and spoiled. When she worked in the office, she was giving orders to employees, and also to Bryce, Jason, and Frank. She had ideas to change how things were done, and she demanded that the changes be made. Frank didn't seem to want to argue with her about it, either," Alec said.

"Why did Frank seem so angry toward Lainey?" I

asked as Lucy passed me the cream. "I had wondered if he was the killer at first."

"Frank is always angry," Alec said with a chuckle. "He was upset that Lainey disappeared after he gave her the job at the farm, and he blames her for dying. He thinks if she would have just stayed here in Sandy Harbor working for him, she would still be alive."

"That's sad, but being there at the farm is what got her killed." I took a sip of my coffee and added more cream.

Lucy sighed. "People go through a whole range of emotions when somebody they love dies. He isn't thinking straight."

I nodded. "They sure do. That was sneaky that Bryce tried to act like it was Jason who had attacked him in order to get the gun from me. I don't know why Jason kept trying to take the gun away, though. If he would have just done what I told him to do, there wouldn't have been any confusion."

"I think it was just an adrenaline reaction," Alec said as he cut into his cheesecake with the side of his fork.

"Adrenaline only tells me to run," Ed said, taking a sip of his black coffee. "It does not tell me to try to take a gun away from a woman who might shoot me."

We all laughed. "I had a lot of adrenaline too," I said. "I might have accidentally shot him. He really wasn't thinking."

Lucy nodded. "I wouldn't have tried to take a gun away from you. Alec, what about the phone calls Ellen Allen was receiving from Lainey's phone?"

"I almost forgot about that," I said. "Jason also said he had called her phone after Christmas and it would ring and ring, until several weeks later when it finally went straight to voicemail."

"Sounds like someone was keeping it charged," Ed said.

Alec took a sip of his coffee before answering. "Bryce had Lainey's phone and purse. He decided to call Ellen because he knew she would tell everyone she was being haunted and he wanted to throw the investigation off. He also lied about seeing Lainey with Jim Martin at the coffee shop to get me to focus on Jim. And the reason no one saw her around town was because he picked her up from the airport when her friend cancelled on her, and he killed her the same day."

I shook my head. "How sad. Why did he bury Lainey out in the blueberry field?"

"He killed her at Christmas time, and there was

snow on the ground, so he covered her with snow, knowing that the field wouldn't be worked for months since it was due to be rested for the coming year. He went out there frequently and checked on things, and when the snow started to melt, he piled more on top to hide her body until he could bury her beneath the blueberry bushes. When he did bury her beneath them, he could only dig a very shallow grave because the ground was still partially frozen."

"That sounds so complicated," I said. "It seems like he could have found another way to get rid of her body."

"I agree. But he figured as long as everybody believed she had just taken off and that she was estranged from the family, they wouldn't go looking for a body. He was right. She wasn't on anybody's radar as a murder victim, and if he had only gone to check on her body after the heavy rains, we probably still wouldn't know that she was dead."

I took a bite of cheesecake and it was just as cool, sweet, and creamy as it should be. I swallowed. "I feel so sorry for their parents, especially Grace. She's such a sweet woman, and she doesn't deserve for this to happen to her."

Alec nodded. "Yes, I spoke to her, and she's broken

up over all of this. Jason was very upset too, as he and Lainey were close. He wasn't close to his brother, and he said he hates him now."

I shook my head and took a sip of my coffee. What an awful end to the summer. "I'm glad Eli had nothing to do with her murder. I don't understand why Bryce and Dave lied about him, though. He would still be working on the farm if they hadn't."

"I think Bryce was worried that Eli might have known more than he let on about Bryce's anger toward Lainey, so he made Eli's life miserable at the farm in the hopes he would quit. After Lainey was found, he tried to blame the murder on him. And Dave just never liked Eli. When Bryce started in on Eli, Dave jumped in too. Allie, this cheesecake is delicious," Alec said.

"So, this was a planned murder?" Lucy asked. "He knew he was going to do it when he picked her up at the airport?"

"Bryce swears it wasn't planned. He said Lainey wanted to meet him in that field to talk in private because she didn't want their parents to overhear their conversation. She told Bryce she was returning to Sandy Harbor and that they should take over the farm and allow their parents to retire early. But

Bryce didn't want her to return to the farm; he wanted her to go back to Oregon. They got into an argument, and he had that small crowbar. He said before he knew what he was doing, he raised it up to her. She saw what he intended to do, turned, and tried to run, and he hit her in the back of the head. He swears he didn't mean to do it. But I don't buy the story that she wanted to meet him out there in that field. They could have met at a coffee shop or someplace else. And it's not like Frank and Grace had Bryce's house bugged. They could have talked there."

"So he did intend to kill her," Ed said. "He lured her out to that field and killed her because he was afraid of her taking over the farm."

Alec nodded. "That's what I believe happened. I'm sure the conversation went the way he said it did, but he either killed her someplace else and took her body out there, or he lured her out there and killed her, as you said."

I sighed and took a bite of cheesecake. Jealousy was a killer. So was sibling rivalry. But my heart still went out to Grace. She had lost two children. One was lost to a sibling, and the other was lost to the state prison system.

I looked at Lucy. "I'm really in the mood for some pumpkin spice yumminess."

She grinned. "Me too. I heard the weatherman say the temps were lowering and fall is right around the corner."

I could hardly wait.

The End

SIGN up to receive my newsletter for updates on new releases and sales:

https://www.subscribepage.com/kathleen-suzette

Follow me on Facebook:

https://www.facebook.com/Kathleen-Suzette-Kate-Bell-authors-759206390932120

BOOKS BY KATHLEEN SUZETTE:

A PUMPKIN HOLLOW CANDY
STORE MYSTERY

Treats, Tricks, and Trespassing
Gumdrops, Ghosts, and Graveyards
Confections, Clues, and Chocolate

A FRESHLY BAKED COZY MYSTERY SERIES

Apple Pie a la Murder

Trick or Treat and Murder

Thankfully Dead

Candy Cane Killer

Ice Cold Murder

Love is Murder

Strawberry Surprise Killer

Plum Dead

Red, White, and Blue Murder

Mummy Pie Murder

Wedding Bell Blunders

In a Jam

Tarts and Terror

Fall for Murder

Web of Deceit

Silenced Santa

New Year, New Murder

Murder Supreme

Peach of a Murder

Sweet Tea and Terror

Die for Pie

Gnome for Halloween

Christmas Cake Caper

Valentine Villainy

Cupcakes and Beaches

Cinnamon Roll Secrets

Pumpkin Pie Peril

Dipped in Murder

A Pinch of Homicide

Layered Lies

Cake and Criminals

Summer's Sweet Demise

A COOKIE'S CREAMERY MYSTERY

Ice Cream, You Scream
Murder with a Cherry on top
Murderous 4th of July
Murder at the Shore
Merry Murder
A Scoop of Trouble
Lethal Lemon Sherbet
Berry Deadly Delight
Chilled to the Cone
Sundae Suspects
Stars, Stripes, and Secrets

A LEMON CREEK MYSTERY

Murder at the Ranch
The Art of Murder
Body on the Boat

A Pumpkin Hollow Mystery Series

Candy Coated Murder
Murderously Sweet
Chocolate Covered Murder
Death and Sweets
Sugared Demise
Confectionately Dead
Hard Candy and a Killer
Candy Kisses and a Killer

Terminal Taffy

Fudgy Fatality

Truffled Murder

Caramel Murder

Peppermint Fudge Killer

Chocolate Heart Killer

Strawberry Creams and Death

Pumpkin Spice Lies

Sweetly Dead

Deadly Valentine

Death and a Peppermint Patty

Sugar, Spice, and Murder

Candy Crushed

Trick or Treat

Frightfully Dead

Candied Murder

Christmas Calamity

A RAINEY DAYE COZY MYSTERY SERIES

Clam Chowder and a Murder

A Short Stack and a Murder

Cherry Pie and a Murder

Barbecue and a Murder

Birthday Cake and a Murder

Hot Cider and a Murder

Roast Turkey and a Murder

Gingerbread and a Murder

Fish Fry and a Murder

Cupcakes and a Murder

Lemon Pie and a Murder

Pasta and a Murder

Chocolate Cake and a Murder

Pumpkin Spice Donuts and a Murder
Christmas Cookies and a Murder
Lollipops and a Murder
Picnic and a Murder
Wedding Cake and a Murder

Made in the USA
Las Vegas, NV
16 August 2024

93933422R00121